THE BOOK OF SHEFFIELD

For Jill, Leigh, and Miles
And in memory of our parents

First published in Great Britain in 2019 by Comma Press.
commapress.co.uk

A CIP catalogue record of this book is available from the British Library.
ISBN: 1912697130
ISBN-13: 978-1-91269-713-7

The publisher gratefully acknowledges assistance from Arts Council England.

Supported using public funding by
**ARTS COUNCIL
ENGLAND**

Printed and bound in England by Clays Ltd, Elcograf S.p.A

The Book of
Sheffield

Edited by Catherine Taylor

Contents

Introduction

'THIS TOWN OF SHEFFIELD is very populous and large,
the streets narrow, and the houses dark and black,
occasioned by the continued smoke of the forges,
which are always at work: Here they make all sorts of
cutlery-ware, but especially that of edged-tools, knives,
razors, axes, and nails.'

So Daniel Defoe recorded in his *A Tour of the Whole Island of
Great Britain,* published in 1724. The author of *Robinson
Crusoe,* probably the first realistic English-language novel, is
one of many literary figures to have passed through Sheffield,
and to document their initial impressions for posterity.

Perhaps the most famous of these is George Orwell's
damning report from *The Road to Wigan Pier* (1937), his survey
of the living and working conditions in the industrial north
just prior to the Second World War.

'Sheffield, I suppose, could justly claim to be called the
ugliest town in the Old World [...] At night, when you
cannot see the hideous shapes of the houses and the
blackness of everything, a town like Sheffield assumes a
kind of sinister magnificence. Sometimes the drifts of
smoke are rosy with sulphur, and serrated flames, like
circular saws, squeeze themselves out from beneath the

cowls of the foundry chimneys. Through the open doors of foundries you see fiery serpents of iron being hauled to and fro by redlit boys, and you hear the whizz and thump of steam hammers and the scream of the iron under the blow.'

No wonder Sheffielders have been fuming and chuckling in equal measure ever since at the Eton-educated Orwell's apparent indictment of their city. Yet Orwell does not completely do Sheffield a disservice, ultimately because of the magnetism of his subject and his prose. Dark Satanic mills aside (and he froths entertainingly on these at some length in *Wigan Pier*, as well as making serious points about dangerous work practices, unsanitary housing and smog-filled air), his descriptions of 'the sinister magnificence' of the city, the 'rosy sulphur' of the smoke, the 'fiery serpents of iron' and the 'redlit boys' have an immediate visual impact, recalling the paintings of the visionary William Blake in all their fevered energy and colour. It also attests to the appeal – which Orwell found 'macabre' – of this 'strange country' of 'the North'.

When, in 1959, the architectural historian Nikolaus Pevsner came to research Sheffield (then in the West Riding of Yorkshire) in his county-by-county guide to Britain, his perspective reached further, observing that 'none of the cities of England has such majestic surroundings'. Encircled by the gritstone quarries and plateaux of the Peak District, its grinding stones or grindstones would play a leading role in the city's steel production and contribute to its rapid growth during the 19th century, leading to the granting of its city charter in 1893. Today, the Peak District National Park remains a major draw for walkers and climbers.

Sheffield takes its name from the River Sheaf, part of a confluence of three rivers including the Loxley and Don. This unique position made it an ideal location for the development of the water-powered industries dating back to its early settlements as well as the deep coal mining which transformed rural communities. The steep decline of both, aided and abetted by successive governments, began in the early 1970s, coincidentally around the time my family moved to the city – first to Crosspool, then Ranmoor, Ecclesall, and Broomhill. By this time the dark satanic mills which Orwell found so menacing had been subject to the establishment of smokeless zones brought into law by the Clean Air Act of 1956; by 1972 the whole of Sheffield had followed suit. However, the industries which had employed generations of workers – mining and steel manufacturing – had also been severely curtailed.

The Sheffield I grew up in was a city on the downturn, in part triggered by the 1973 OPEC oil crisis and the redistribution of steel production in Europe. It's worth considering how rapid that sliding scale seems in the light of its overall history. Although Sheffield is often considered a 'product' of the industrial revolution, it has been at the centre of blade production since the time of Chaucer – by 1600 the city was the largest producer of cutlery outside London. Before the domination of the factories, which managed larger steel production (and later stainless-steel alloy, discovered and patented from 1912), self-employed master craftsmen, known as Little Mesters, would produce, from multiple tiny workshops, the hand-made edge tools for which Sheffield became famous. Perhaps this, along with its parks and street trees, is a factor behind Sheffield's claim that it is 'the biggest village in the world'.

And it is a city of contrasts: starkly drawn in the 1970s and 80s, with the affluent western suburbs (praised by the poet John Betjeman as 'the prettiest' in the country) and imposing civic buildings belying the grimmer image of a dour steel- and cutlery-making centre and the sprawl of post-war high-rise to the east. Today, Sheffield looks forward to a post-post-industrial future. A new generation of Little Mesters – artists and artisans – have workspaces in former factories; the Park Hill estate is Grade II listed and used for everything from the filming of the *Dr Who* television series to conceptual art installations. The Victorian glasshouses in the Botanical Gardens have been given an overhaul thanks to National Lottery funding, as has Sheffield city centre; the old General Cemetery, one of the first garden cemeteries in the UK on its creation in 1836, has restored its imposing non-conformist chapel, where as a teenager I would spend hours sitting on its crumbling steps, illicitly smoking cigarettes and reading poetry out loud.

Yet it remains a city of divisions and protest - from the early Chartist movement of the 1830s to the 1983-84 miners' strike and the recent campaign to stop the felling of thousands of its street trees, to the most hotly debated topic of the last few years – Brexit. The decision of Sheffield to vote Leave (the only major northern city to do so) in the 2016 referendum – by 52 to 48%, the same margin as the UK overall – laid bare the understandable feelings of decades of disappointment and neglect wielded by governments perceived as uncaring and elitist. Despite all the lottery funding and investment from overseas, there are parts of the city that look the same as when I was a child in the 1970s; even some that Orwell would recognise from the late 1930s. People talk of the north/south divide, but that fracture exists in this city, too.

And Sheffield certainly provides rich pickings for writers, as is clear from the ten wonderfully different stories which make up this book. The General Cemetery is the evocative backdrop for 'Born on Sunday, Silent', Désirée Reynolds's powerful story of the grave of an African child dating from the early 1900s, and the city's shameful collusion in a racist and imperial past.

Margaret Drabble, who was born in Sheffield just before the outbreak of the Second World War, while reflecting on family and loss in 'The Avenue' also places the concerns of the current #MeToo movement in an ambiguous moment at the Crucible Theatre in the 1970s. Karl Riordan's 'Scrap', about the exploits of a pair of inept petty thieves, set during the desperation of the 1980s' recession, is both funny and poignant. Naomi Frisby writes of regret and resilience in 'The Time is Now', her story of the break-up of both a band and a love affair. Told retrospectively, it contains Angela Carter-esqe elements of surprise. Ghosts seep into Gregory Norminton's elegiac tale of ecology, migrancy and longing, 'How to Love What Dies', and Geoff Nicholson's unsettling 'The Father Figure', where a man repeatedly encounters the recently dead father about whom he had felt deeply ambivalent in life.

The eve of the millennium and an evening's clubbing which may or may not be a disaster in the making is the background to Johny Pitts's winning, effervescent 'Like a Night Out in Sheffield'; Philip Hensher gives us a wickedly funny and dark account of a sixteen-year-old just coming to terms with his sexuality while involved with a questionable political group in an extract from his forthcoming novel *A Small Revolution in Germany*; Tim Etchells, in a breath-taking piece of metafiction, examines an alternative dystopian England – Endland – with Sheffield at its centre, in 'Long Fainting/Try Saving Again'; and Helen Mort brings her poet's eye to the superb 'Weaning' which maps the terrain of the city and its environs onto the landscape of the body of a woman after the birth of her child. Ten stories and ten look-out points from which to gaze down at the ever-changing Steel City in all its manifestations.

Catherine Taylor
October, 2019

Weaning

Helen Mort

SHE WAS LOSING THE names of places. Every time she dropped a feed, let the milk in her breasts come then lessen, another part of the city disappeared. Someone once said Sheffield was a dirty picture in a golden frame. She was forgetting both; the town and the gritstone encircling it. One bright Sunday, she walked out past The Norfolk Arms and the black clutch of the plantation. The baby sat upright in the heather with his chubby legs splayed, shoving strawberries into his mouth and letting the juice trickle down his chin. She ate nothing, tried to count the green tower blocks in her line of vision. Gleadless. She said it out loud so she would not forget. Her husband phoned; his voice steady with concern.

'Where are you?'

'We've gone for a walk.'

'Where?'

'The place where I climb. The big rocks. Beside the car park.'

Later, she learned that it was Burbage. They had a map in the house, inherited from her father-in-law and she circled it in biro, marked a neat X.

★

As the weeks passed, the map became a maze of noughts and crosses. Attercliffe. Meersbrook. Norton. She pinned it to the wall of the bedroom with Blu-Tack and when the baby slept, she could run her palm flat over it, feel the indentations of the pen, trace an inventory of her loss. Other names were stubbornly recalled. Meadowhall. Don Valley. Owlerton. When she was a teenager, she used to kill time thumbing through the records in Rare and Racy on Devonshire Green even though her parents owned no record player. On the wall was a framed map of Sheffield bomb sites. The black circles looked like bullet holes. The map seemed to have more dots than spaces. Her grid of the city was starting to feel like that. The shop was gone now, and she wondered what had happened to all the records.

★

One morning, she woke up with the word Heeley on her tongue. She had been dreaming of the City Farm, the sturdy legs of the goats that crowded by the fence and lunged for scraps, alert and noisy, the smell of wet straw and new rain, the farmyard cat which stalked between the pens. By lunchtime, Heeley had gone and she was forced to find the road on the map, the place she knew the farm was. The health visitor called round while she was unloading bags of shopping from the car.

'Is this a good time?'

They drank lukewarm tea from mugs decorated with pictures of biscuits. The health visitor's said *I Know How To Party* underneath a drawing of a pink frosted party ring. The health visitor asked her about the crying spells and how long they lasted, whether she was getting enough sleep. The health visitor did not ask about the place names and their slow vanishing. The health visitor nodded earnestly and kept her hands folded in her lap.

'The way you feel is nothing to do with weaning, with

2

breastfeeding,' she said. 'You're looking for something to blame.'

The health visitor left her with the address of an Australian website offering Cognitive Behavioural Therapy. A gym for moods. You had to pay. Then you had to answer a series of questions. They were called Initial Questions. She scrolled through them on her phone at night but none of them seemed relevant. The only important question now was, where am I?

★

She had taken to falling asleep holding her son's snowsuit. It was maroon-coloured with a fur trim and it had only fitted him for a short time when he was a newborn and his head still flopped. Now, at night, she clutched it and imagined him older in the snow, pictured him toddling through all the white-covered, quiet places of the city, the parks now nameless to her. She thought of his footprints in the woods by the side of the stream. There were crossing places, rough stones that dogs scampered over, low overhanging branches. There was a memorial to a plane that came down here decades ago, crashing into the bank. There were climbing frames and silver slides and swings where children squealed to be pushed higher. There were places for sliding, families dragging sledges obediently up the slopes. How could she keep her son safe and near if she did not know where he was walking? She took the map down and shone the light of her phone on it, haloing the script, the roads and boundaries. Endcliffe Park. Bingham Park. Whiteley Woods. She circled every one obediently.

★

When he fed from the bottle, her baby was meek as a small lamb or a piglet, swallowing quietly, the formula milk running down his chin. She sat him in the crook of her arm and kissed the top of his head as she tilted the teat towards his mouth. The tablets were making her wake at 2am, 3am. Her heart skittered.

Outside, foxes made their low, catastrophic noises, ran along the tops of fences, skirted over walls and vanished into the last secret places of suburbia.

★

She read articles: 'The Hardest Eight Weeks of My Life' and 'What Nobody Told Me About Oxytocin'. She scrolled through advice on stopping breastfeeding, found only support to continue. But mostly, she read the map, running her finger from left to right and from top to bottom, following the course of the A57 out through Broomhill and Crosspool, skirting Rivelin and curving towards Strines. She could remember driving out to Ladybower, misjudging the bends and taking them too quickly, watching the wire hair and rust of the moors easing into view.

Standing before the full-length mirror, she found her breasts had disappeared altogether. For the last six months, they had been swollen with milk, pale blue veins standing out under her skin. Now, her profile had flattened. Her nipples were the colour of freckles. She dropped her t-shirt to the floor and ran a hand down from her collarbone to her navel the way she touched the map. Her body was Sheffield. She would have to learn it again.

★

From the top, of their road she could see the south side of town. In Sheffield you could always get a view of somewhere else, always get up high enough to look across the rooftops. Still, she sought out elevated places. The Greystones pub with its tarmac, makeshift beer garden. The Brothers Arms. The high point of the General Cemetery. Each of her journeys was charted, noted on the map with a spidery, faint line lest she forget it. At home, her phone buzzed with messages.

You should breastfeed again. He's still so tiny.

You should stop gradually.

4

You should stop quickly if you're going to do it. Like pulling off a plaster.

It's hormones.

It's sleep deprivation.

It's emotional.

You're grieving for your child.

She deleted the mood gym. She stopped texting friends back. When that wasn't enough, she drove down Abbeydale Road South, out through Totley to Owler Bar and then across to Barbrook. She left the car in the lay-by and walked the deep groove of the track out to the little reservoir. There were aimless ducks and the remnants of disposable barbecues, patches of blackened grass. A lone swimmer was making pitiful progress through the weed and peaty sludge, his face set with determination. She crouched by the side of the bank and cupped her hands around her phone and released it into the water as if she were returning a frog to the wild. It slipped easily into the darkness and was gone. On the way back, she visited the stone circle. A flattened ring of twelve squat stones, angled towards each other, their conversation long since interrupted. She consulted her map to know what surrounded her. Ramsley Moor and Big Moor. Then the unnamed things, the indifferent sky and the slow planes.

★

She began to enjoy the way her son handled food, his detachment and curiosity. He would lift raspberries into the air and repeatedly scrunch them between his fingers, only putting them towards his mouth as an afterthought. When she gave him strips of bread, he sometimes chewed on them but just as often raised them and let them drop ceremoniously. Crusts gathered on the kitchen floor. Then he would grin his toothless smile and grunt. There was joy in the letting go. He loved to throw squiggles of pasta, to flatten his hands in peanut butter. She took him to cafes in the city centre where he flung the mango and avocado she'd so carefully sliced and packed in a plastic tub on the ground to be squashed and trodden, oozing juice into the reclaimed boards. Nobody ever minded. Everybody smiled at his smeared face, the blobs of food on his nose and forehead.

★

On the last day of the eighth week, she bundled her baby into a sling and set off from Lady's Bridge, checking the map as she went, not for directions but for place names. There was a spidery footbridge, metal and tall. The Cobweb Bridge. Her footsteps echoed on it. The walls were pink and green with graffiti. She could follow the Five Weirs Walk all the way past the industrial estates and then walk back along the canal to the basin. It was a grey, humid morning and she was sweating already. There were diversions and footpath closures and the route sent her past old foundries and sleepy sandwich shops with chalkboards outside. She could hear welding, men shouting over the din. Somehow, just when it seemed she would never rejoin the water it would appear, rushing constant on her left. Attercliffe, a proud bridge, the weir running silver. By the shopping precinct, she took her baby out of the carrier and leaned him forwards towards the sound. A heron appeared to their right, stepping thoughtfully from depth to shallows. Her son squealed and flapped his arm, bird-like and sudden. There were shopping trolleys and tyres, lengths of orange rope. Life was everywhere around them, endless and derelict and broken. It did not matter, she thought, what any of this was called. It was all pure river.

The Avenue

Margaret Drabble

'This lime tree bower my prison'

EVERY TIME SHE WENT back to Sheffield she revisited The
Avenue, where she had spent the long intensity of her
childhood years. She was drawn back to it, irresistibly, back
to its pollarded and stumpy lime trees, its grassy verges, its
semi-detached houses, its blue suburban skies, its repository
of angst and longing. Her family had left The Avenue long
ago and most of the people she had known there were dead.
Her only brother had died there, at the age of sixteen, and
her parents had died years later in southern Sidmouth, their
soft retirement home. The unassuming Sheffield street had
been marked by tragedy and loss, and she had fled from it as
soon as she could, as a student to Bristol (how shockingly
different that city had seemed to her, and how wonderfully
liberated the Bristol Old Vic and its acolytes), then to weekly
rep in Salisbury, then on to London and the Old Vic and the
West End and White City, and, occasionally, to Broadway.
And once, unhappily, to Hollywood, which had proved a
flight too far. Her Yorkshire self drew the line at the excesses
of Hollywood. But however far she journeyed, she was
always caught on a loop of returning. She could never resist
an invitation to Sheffield. And here she was again, possibly for
the last time.

She was always saying that phrase to herself, 'possibly for the last time', in her private melodramatic manner, but the last time had not yet come. You think it must be the end, but it is not the end, as Samuel Beckett once said. Or something to that effect.

She had watched Sheffield change dramatically, as it rose from the ashes of its bomb sites and reached for the skies with cheese graters and egg boxes and wedding cakes, and created fountains and arches and winter gardens, and defiantly declared itself a nuclear-free zone. But The Avenue changed not at all. It remained stubbornly itself, a backwater, a residential mixture of Edwardian and 1930s detached and semi-detached houses. Decade after decade, she had walked its ways. And here she was again, on a long summer evening, 'possibly for the last time'. Here were the lime trees, their little winged fruits fluttering and circling down to the pavement, as they had always done.

The occasions of her returns had been as motley and as various as her career and as the changing cityscape, occasions that had altered over time. An old school friend's wedding, a teacher's retirement party, an honorary degree, a television series, a dinner at the Cutlers' Hall, the opening of an arts centre, a documentary biopic. Most happily, most rewardingly, she had several times played The Crucible, a theatre which had not existed in her childhood and which, over more than forty years, had earned itself a fine reputation. With dazzling panache, it had united art and sport, and had become famous not only for Arthur Miller and Dennis Potter and Rony Robinson and Victoria Wood but also for snooker. She had never learned the rules of snooker, but she was happy that it existed and would occasionally watch a dramatic late-night shoot out after the show as she lay sleepless in a lonely hotel. A dual-use theatre had been an inspired concept. Snooker, incomprehensible though it was, made her feel at home.

Her favourite stage role at The Crucible had been Masha in *The Three Sisters*, some time in the early 1980s. She had been a little old for the part but had not looked it. Melancholy yearning had been one of her stocks in trade, and her Masha, dressed in black and 'in mourning for her life', had been memorable, to herself and to others. She had felt at home with Masha's elegant grief. On the last night the actor playing opposite her, as they embraced for their final parting kiss, had put his tongue right into her mouth. This was against all the rules. She had been astonished at this comic and indefensible act of transgression, this sudden overstepping of the bounds of make-believe. She'd never been sure if it had been deliberate or impulsive. She remembered it now, as she once more paced The Avenue, 'possibly for the last time'. She remembered the muscular roughness of Jack Barnett's tongue, and wondered whether her surprise had been visible to the audience. What response had he hoped to provoke? The incident had never been mentioned between them, or by her to anyone, and by chance she had never worked with him again. That startling French kiss remained a meaningless enigma. She hadn't thought of it for years.

But she knew what had prompted the memory. It was that question, this morning, about #MeToo.

The world of theatre and film had changed so much during her long career, which had been launched at a time when stage plays were still subjected to the approval of the Lord Chamberlain, who diligently and ridiculously deleted expletives and references to sexual deviance and the Royal Family. His powers had long been removed, and stage and screen nudity and simulated sexual activity had become professionally acceptable and for some actors *de rigueur*. And now we were all living in the risky world of #MeToo. She had been carefully avoiding questions from the press about it, but had been caught unawares that morning by a question in a live interview for Radio Sheffield, and had found herself mumbling and blundering as she tried to avoid a direct answer. The interviewer, a ginger-haired lad called Joe, had been charmingly, disarmingly friendly, and she hadn't seen the subject coming. She wanted to say that she had never been exploited, that she knew how to draw her own boundaries, that she could always give as good as she got, that she didn't think much of women who stayed silent for twenty years and then jumped on a bandwagon to dress up in black dresses for the Oscars. Black dresses with deep cleavages, what a statement, what a mixed message. But she hadn't had the guts. She had mumbled and prevaricated and said how much respect she had for everybody and tried to change the topic. Joe had been gentle and let her off the hook. Although of Viking ancestry, like many Yorkshiremen (as he'd told her, having had a recent DNA test for a fortieth birthday present), he wasn't in for the kill.

Pacing The Avenue, on a summer evening, she realised it had never occurred to her until this day that Jack's kiss could have been an act of aggression. An insult. She hadn't even thought of thinking about it in those terms. Had the time come when one had to rewrite the whole of the past?

In the studio they'd agreed to abandon the subject of #MeToo, and talked instead about her earliest childhood memories of theatre in Sheffield. She told Joe that her family were not theatre goers, in those pre-Crucible days. (She had said all this many times in interviews before, but it seemed more meaningful to talk about it here, and Joe made a good show of pretending he'd never heard any of it. As maybe he hadn't. He was only a lad.) They'd gone only once a year, at Christmas, on a ritual outing with the family next door, to the pantomime at The Lyceum. How she had loved it! The glitter, the glamour, the red velvet and the gilded chandeliers, the cross-dressing, the flying ballet, the high-kicking chorus girls with their brown legs and their fish-net tights and their glowing Five and Nine faces! Yes, she had fallen in love with the swish of the curtain and the smell of the greasepaint in those early years, but no, she had never appeared or even been asked to appear in a panto! 'I was always more of a tragedy queen,' she had demurred, with a conciliatory and self-deprecating little laugh.

And there had also been the excitement of sitting next to her brother Eliot's best friend, Nick. Nick, the Boy Next Door.

She hadn't told Joe about Nick, he was too hard to explain, but she was thinking about him now, intensely, as she sat herself down upon a slightly sticky wooden seat under one of the larger trees, holding a sprig of pale green winged lime seeds in her hand. (A metal plaque on the bench said: 'In Memory of Patricia Spalding, who loved The Avenue.' Patricia Spalding, whoever she was, had been after her day.) Nick and Eliot had been passionately interested in the theatre, in opera, in music, in literature. They were close. They were always in and out of one another's houses and gardens and bedrooms. They co-authored plays and operas and libretti and wrote admiring reviews of their own works in the style of Harold Hobson and Kenneth Tynan. They'd been writing plays together even before they reached adolescence, and occasionally condescended to ask her to play a part. So her first acting roles had been premiered in The Avenue. A princess, a witch, a goddess. Her favourite part was Andromeda, chained to the end of a brass bedstead in the spare bedroom. Nick and Eliot had alternated as the ravening Sea Monster and her saviour, Perseus. She couldn't remember any of the lines, but she could remember the mood of the little drama – violent, highfalutin, wordy, and, as she now recognised, erotic. A ravished maiden draped in a white sheet and chained to a rock as a sacrifice. An archetypal victim. #MeToo wouldn't have liked that at all, but she had loved it. Though, even at the time, she had realised that

Nick and Eliot were far more into one another than they were into her. She was just an accessory.

That hadn't bothered her at all. She could look after herself, then as now. But Eliot's early death of leukaemia (an even worse illness in those days than it was now) had profoundly affected her parents, herself and Nick Armitage, the Boy Next Door. She had slowly come to acknowledge that it was her mother's unassuageable grief that had led to her being resolutely childless. She'd never wanted children. It wasn't her career that had been the obstacle (though fitting children into a theatrical life was never very easy for anyone) but the thought of the possibility of having to endure bereavement. She'd watched it, and she didn't want to go there. (That's how she put it to herself now, though that strangely apposite phrase hadn't been available to her in earlier years. It was a useful coinage, unlike some.) She had (as she came slowly to perceive) externalised her fear of loss into her interpretation of sombre or tragic roles... Masha, Cordelia, Hedda, Electra, Miss Julie, Rose Aylmer, Eurydice, she'd done them all. Tragedy queen, as she'd joked this morning to ginger-haired Joe.

Joe had told her that his DNA Birthday Kit had told him he was mostly Viking but 1% 'Eskimo'. How odd was that?

The only time in adult life that she'd met the Boy Next Door she had sensed that he had found her career choice vulgar, her worldly success vulgar. His own success had been so esoteric that she had struggled to come to terms with it. She'd noted while flipping through the *Sunday Times* one autumn morning in the 1970s that someone named Nicholas Armitage had published a novel called *Cemetery Road*, and a brief glance at the review had confirmed that this was their own Nick, for the book was set in Sheffield. The word 'Sheffield' always leaped from the page at her, however uninteresting the news story, and, coupled with the name of Nicholas Armitage, it was not to be missed. She hadn't actually read it, though she'd looked at it in a bookshop, but a glance or two had told her that it was not for her. It was pretentious, sparse and abstract, and didn't seem to have much of a story line. It had been dedicated to E.M, which she assumed meant her brother Eliot, though there didn't seem to be anything about him in the book. It had won a prize in France, where it had been acclaimed as an English *nouveau roman*. And Nicholas had made good on this debut with a string of fictions, essays, and critical biographies, earning himself a sound reputation as a writer of the avant-garde. She didn't know what the terms 'structuralist' and 'post-modern' meant, they had come in after her time, but he was associated with whatever it was that they were. She assumed he had a proper day job, in teaching or in publishing. He couldn't have made a living out of rarefied fiction and literary journalism.

He'd got in touch with her some thirty years ago, through her agent, and invited her to lunch. He had written a play, he told her, and would like her to have a look at it. There might be a part in it for her. She got quite a few letters like that in those days, when she was on an upward trajectory, and although she doubted if he could have written anything that would suit her, she couldn't resist the opportunity of setting eyes upon him, after all these years. He suggested lunch at the once-celebrated Wheeler's, a London fish restaurant that was already past its best, and there they met, just off Piccadilly, at a table in a little Edwardian alcove draped with rather shabby red velvet, and laid with heavy silver cutlery and heavily embossed white napkins.

He had grown a little goatee beard and he was very thin. He wore a waistcoat. For a Modernist, he looked a little old-fashioned. And faintly Mephistophelean.

He seemed unnaturally confident that she would like his script. She had glanced at it and had noted that the part he had suggested for her, that of Madame O, was not only mystifying but rather short. Not enough lines, a basic defect in a drama.

He ordered sole Veronique, an old-fashioned if classic dish. The peeled green grapes surrounding the white fish were translucent and very slightly sinister. Like pale eyes drowning.

They did not mention Eliot or speak much of their conjoined childhood. They stuck to the present, to matters in hand, to their career choices. She was disconcerted by his manner, which seemed to suggest that she was the supplicant, not he. He manoeuvred her into the slightly ridiculous and defensive position of insisting how busy she was, how packed her schedule. She could tell that he was adept at wrong-footing people. Not, she would have thought, a good technique for procuring favours.

But there they had been together in London, in a chic though faded restaurant, the two grown-up children from The Avenue. It had been a bizarre luncheon, out of time.

And here she was, back in The Avenue, sitting on a bench outside Number 36. That's where Tim and Anne Drury had lived, long ago. On summer evenings like this, the children of The Avenue had emerged after tea to play games on the grass verge. Truth or Dare. Blind Man's Buff, Kiss and Tell, jacks, conkers. On the pavement they had played hopscotch, with bits of slate, on a grid chalked out with a flinty stone. There were no children playing now. Fewer and fewer children played street games. They had been scared off by the Yorkshire Ripper and pollution; they had been lured away by television and tablets.

She was thinking about Nick Armitage, she was summoning up his ghost. And here he came, the revenant, right on cue. She heard him before she saw him. Tap, tap, tap, on the pavement, shuffling along The Avenue like Blind Pew, with a little cane.

Was he blind? Would he see her? Did he too haunt The Avenue, over the years?

He looked much the same as when she'd last seen him, long ago in the Edwardian restaurant, though even thinner, and a little smaller, and more withered. The same little goatee beard, the same dapper clothes. A silver-grey jacket, a dove grey shirt, a pale blue tie.

He came slowly, walking delicately. Tap, tap, tap, deliberately, as though he enjoyed the mildly menacing acoustics of his approach. Should she speak to him? If she didn't speak, would he just tap his way past and disappear out of the frame?

He paused when he was within earshot.

'Nick?' she said.

Yes, he knew she was there, he had spotted her. He was neither lame nor blind.

He took a few more steps, tap, tap, tap on the hopscotch pavement. He stopped, and took her in, as she sat there in her black summer dress, with the pale yellow-green wings of the lime on her knee.

An unexpected flow of benevolence and forgiveness of the sadness of the past filled her.

She patted the bench, beckoned him, indicated that he should come to sit by her.

Silently, he approached, and silently he took his place, with a sardonic but not unfriendly little smile.

Silently, they sat together, side by side.

There was nothing they could say that could bridge the years. So they said nothing.

The Avenue is always the same. It transfixes time. It is the deep well of memory. They sit there in silence, side by side, as it were forever. They are their own effigies.

Like a Night out in Sheffield

Johny Pitts

'CAN I SEE YOUR NUS card, pal?'

I don't have an NUS card, but Roots Manuva is playing a live gig and I've decided it's time to branch out from the usual. Half of my mates don't even know who Roots Manuva is, the other half think he does soft hip-hop for students who don't really like hip-hop. I tried to convince them to come along by telling them about all the student lasses they were leaving to indie boy art wankers, but they thought that the girls looked like indie art wankers too. That none of them even had tans or showed enough cleavage.

So I left my mates in Empire Bar and decided to give freshers' week a go on me tod. Just behind this bouncer I can see student birds in tank tops and tight bootcut jeans. They're different to the lasses I went to school with. They're into foreign cinema and that, which I've proper been getting into recently. After quitting my GNVQ in construction, before I got my job at B&Q, I'd doss around town and sometimes end up in that Showroom Cinema, like. On certain days you could get in the back entrance, and if you waited until five minutes into the film, no one would see you sneak in. Got into some reight random films; watching the lives of different people on

17

the big screen was an escape from my life, that seemed to be going nowhere fast. I'm 20 now and I've made it my new millennium resolution to expand my world, read books, watch foreign cinema and pull student birds. Speaking of which, the most beautiful lass I've ever seen is paying to get in ahead of me. She looks right like Julie Delpy. Better yet, she turns around and gives me a naughty little smile, so I try my luck with the 6'4" roid-head in front of me one more time.

'Sorry, pal. I'm going to need to see an NUS card.'

Bastard. I tell the arsehole that I'm studying Journalism at Sheffield University, and make up a professor's name. That it's freshers' week and – *stupid me* – I left sending off for my NUS card until the last minute, so it hasn't arrived in the post yet. I proper beg him to let me in and make up a story about all my pals being inside, and that if he'd just let me go in and get one of them, they'd vouch for me. But he doesn't budge an inch, just lets a bunch of posh wankers pass by me, who look like they haven't washed all week. They should want people like me in their club. I'm wearing a pressed white £80 short-sleeved Ben Sherman shirt, £100 pair of Clarks Wallabies, £70 trousers from House of Fraser and £40 leather wrist strap from Brother2Brother. I smell of Paco Rabanne *for him* from Debenhams. Cost me a month's wages all this. My pleas turn into indignation and I tell the bouncer that I'm going to write a piece in the student paper about doormen ruining nights out, directly implicating him if he doesn't let me in. But he just laughs.

'Good luck to you, pal'

Fuck it, I'll go back to Empire Bar. I won't be seeing Roots Manuva tonight, but I might see Julie Delpy in Reppers later.

When I arrive at Empire, there's a queue. There's never a queue at Empire. I wait for ten minutes in the freezing cold only to get in and see that the lads have already moved on. My mates have set routes on a night out, so I know they'll now either be in Po Na Na or Bar Centro. I'm sobering up big time, so I buy two bottles of VK Blue for £1 a piece and neck them in the toilet, because I don't want anyone to see me drinking on my own like Billy No Mates. It's amazing how VK Blue actually makes you more thirsty. They're oreight if you just have one or two; taste like pop, but this is my fourth and fifth, and they're starting to make my teeth feel furry and give me heartburn. They do keep you drunk, though, and I've only got £12 left. Fiver to get into Reppers, then six more VK Blues or VK Apples. An hour's walk home via Greasy Vera's for a 20p tom dip on a bread cake and job's a good 'un. I down the fluorescent blue shit one straight after the other and then head to Po Na Na.

Inside, I don't see any of my mates but I do see Steve from Fitness First. He must be about 50 but dresses like he's 20, has his hair dyed peroxide blonde. I have never done a workout at Fitness First and not seen him in there. He's wearing a skin-tight sleeveless t-shirt - showing off his arms with slightly above average muscles - and these new Nike trainers that look like ninja slippers. He says he saw my mates but they've moved on, and offers me a pint that is three quarters full. He tells me it tastes like shit, but I can finish it if I want.

'Some reight birds out tonight, int there?' he says. Not bad, I say, but add that the bouncers are right bellends. He asks me how weight training is going, and suggests a protein shake that has an ingredient called creatine in it, that makes your arms massive. Steve's mate Mick walks over, who is also a Fitness First legend for using all the machines incorrectly with right bad form. He's gonna do his back in one day this lad. Mick must be about 30 odd, and acts as Steve's wingman and sidekick, and the dynamic duo tell me they're off to Pulse and Cocktails if I want to join them. I can't even get into a club with an 18-age restriction without ID, never mind one where you have to be 21, but I can't be arsed searching all over Sheffield for my pals, so join Steve and Mick. We head for one of those special double decker buses the clubs put on for free, that take you from town to the shiny outlands of 'Centertainment'. If I don't get into Pulse and Cocktails I'll just go on to Club Wow next door.

When I get on the bus, I'm buzzing – that extra pint has tipped me into tipsiness. On the top deck are a bunch of pissed Sheffield United nutters, singing the Greasy Chip Butty song, and I join in on the line 'Like a good pinch of snuff!'

Just when I've come to terms with having the same old night out as usual, I turn around and, sitting behind me, is that reight fit Julie Delpy lass. She smiles and says: 'that bouncer was being such a prick. He let one of my friends in who forgot her NUS.' She's right posh, and in the bright lights of the Club Wow bus I see that she is even fitter that I remembered, with a quality tribal tattoo of a sun with some sort of Asian symbol in it. I tell her it's wicked and she says she got it in Thailand when she was backpacking on her gap year. I ask her if she's seen the film *The Beach* yet – I saw it at the cinema last week and loved it. She says it's shit, that it's nowhere near as good as the book, which she read while she was travelling. I go a bit quiet, then tell her she looks like Julie Delpy, and she beams at me with a smile and says: 'Oh my God, I absolutely love *Before Sunrise,* it's one of my favourite films!' Me too, I say, and tell her I love world cinema. She smiles politely and informs me that 'world cinema' is a problematic, neo-colonial term, because it suggests that English speaking cinema in Britain and America is authentic cinema, and everything else outside that is branded as the 'world'. And in any case, *Before Sunrise* isn't really world cinema.

I don't know what she's on about but tell her she has nice eyes, and then ask if she's ever seen *La Haine*. She rolls her nice eyes and says, 'Who hasn't!' And I think, who *has*? No one else I know. She's literally the first person I've met other than me who's seen it. Then she says, 'You're quite cute aren't you?' and I say, 'I'm not bad, am I?' And she laughs then asks me what I'm studying at Uni. I tell her Journalism, praying she doesn't know anyone studying Journalism, but before she can chuck too many questions my way I throw the same back at her. 'Nothing as practical as journalism – I'm studying Cultural Anthropology.' I don't know what anthropology is, but I say, cool. Julie Delpy smiles. 'I bet you could write some stories about Club Wow. It would definitely be a great place to do anthropology. Maybe we should collaborate on a research project tonight?' As the bus pulls up, I turn to Steve and Mick, and Steve gives me a knowing look and laughs. 'Have a good night, pal. Doing chest and biceps at two tomorrow if you fancy it.' I tell him that I'll see how I feel and leave with Julie Delpy.

When we enter Club Wow, S Club 7's 'S Club Party' is playing. Julie Delpy looks around at the interior, which resembles a giant Fisher Price toy and shouts, 'This place is hilarious,' but I don't find it that hilarious, just a bit wank. 'It's definitely not Roots Manuva,' I shout back, and Julie Delpy gives me a sympathetic smile, but honestly, with Julie Delpy, Club Wow has never seemed so full of promise. The DJ is eclectic, but only because he doesn't really know what he's doing. One minute he's playing Bon Jovi's 'Living on a Prayer', the next he's spinning 2Pac's 'California Love', before going into a bit of Blur, then mainstream UK Garage. He lines up 'Flowers' by Sweet Female Attitude and a burst of multicoloured confetti falls from the ceiling. Julie Delpy looks into my eyes and softly kisses me.

This kiss seems to last forever, and when we break apart I ask her if she wants to go back to her student flat for a shag, but she looks at me, partly in shock, partly in disgust and says that it was 'unbecoming' of me. I don't know what that means, but I know it isn't a yes. Thank God for Ini Kamoze: 'HIT IT: Naaaa na na na Naaah na na na naaaaaah na na naaaaah na na naaaaah' plays and Julie forgets all about my proposal and throws her hands in the air. 'Oh my God this is a fucking classic,' she says, and I shout, 'Baaaad tune!' Julie Delpy grinds into me and I gently put my hands on her waist, above her low-rise jeans, and she doesn't move them away. 'Are you going to try a bit harder on the charm front?' she asks me, but I'm enjoying touching her waist too much to say anything smart or flirty… and just say, 'Er, yeah, sorry.'

All in all it's turning into a great night. After my daft proposal, Julie Delpy's still getting off with me, there's a 2 for 1 special on bottles of Reef and VK Apple, which means when I buy a drink I can offer to buy Julie one too, and roughly every fifth song the DJ plays is something I can dance to. But it's too good to last. Someone shoves into my shoulder, as if wanting to start a feight. I turn around, and can honestly say I've never wanted to see my group of mates less than right now. Daz, my oldest friend, pulls me away and shouts, in full ear shot of Julie Delpy, 'Where the fuck have you been? And who's that student lass wearing shit trainers?' I'm a bit drunk, and tell Daz her name's Julie Delpy, and he turns to the rest of the lads and says, 'He's found mi Julie! Wiiicked man!' in a scarily good Ali G voice, which makes him seem like even more of a bellend. Daz carries on; 'Mate, reight funny. Smithy smacked this kid in Reppers, we got booted out and ended up in Berlins, then I got off with that Kirsty bird who works in House of Fraser make-up department. You like that don't you!' Then he turns to Julie Delpy, 'Any how, love, has this sneaky little bastard been telling you he's studying journalism? It's true. You should see his award-winning reporting on broken kitchen tiles on aisle four!' All the other lads laugh then look at me. I move them on by offering to buy some VK blues, and ask Julie if she wants me to bring her one back. She says she's alright.

I tell Daz that he's cock-blocking (this is the only phrase that will make Daz honourably fuck off) and that I'll meet him at the bar in a bit, and Julie Delpy moves close to my ear and asks, 'Who are these tossers?' I tell her they're just some old school friends. 'You'd better go and have a drink with them then,' she says in a way that is more order than suggestion. I tell her I'll be back in five minutes, and Daz puts his arms around me, tells me that I could do better, and buys us all a round of black Sambuca shots. I'm eager to get back to Julie Delpy, but Daz – who makes more money than all of us as a plumber – keeps plowing us with black Sambuca… and it takes overr… th nihgt n… am… pisedd as fcuk…

Where am I? Where's Julie Delpy? What was her real name again? Did I even find out? The cold wind is sobering me up. Shit, did I get thrown out for being too drunk? I'm in Attercliffe somewhere. Oh yes, I have to walk home. Centertainment is much closer to Wincobank, where I live. I can do it. I climb and fall up the bastard of a hill that is Jenkin Road and have a rest on a bench when I finally get to the top. I sniff my trousers to see if they've aired out a bit and I'll be able to get another wear out of them because it says on the label they're dry clean only. Will I eck – they reek of second hand smoke. The soles of my Clarks are sticky with alcopop residue from Club Wow's dance floor. I check my pockets: a 50 pence piece, an unused extra sensitive Durex condom, my provisional driver's license, and in my back pocket a Sheffield Mainline bus ticket. Something's written on it. To my amazement there's an 0114 number on it and the words 'Julie Delpy :)' scrawled over it!

My head's spinning but from this bench on top of Jenkin

Hill I can see an almost 360 degree panoramic view of Sheffield, from Park Hill flats through all the old factories that most of my family used to work at, and right over to Meadowhall shopping centre, where most of my family work now. But Sheffield has never seemed so luminous and full of possibility. BT Phone booths glow like Japanese lanterns, street lamps shine like fire flies, bathing Fisto and Oner 007 pieces (that tonight seem like masterpieces) in a sepia glow. Proper beautiful. I wonder if I'll ever leave this place? If I'll ever go backpacking around Thailand like Julie Delpy? I think that's why I watch world cinema. Er, I mean cinema made outside of English speaking places. Cause even if I can't afford it in real life, I can travel through space and time, and breathe, and turn B&Q into a sun drenched day-dream. God, I really do stink of cigarettes.

Visiting the Radicals

Philip Hensher

WE HAD CROSSED THE dual carriageway. We skirted the railway station, walking up into the landscape of orange lights, half of them broken, and rancid concrete doorways, deep in shadow, that constituted the Park Hill estate. There was nobody about. It was hard not to feel some fear. I had never been there before. The others were talking too loudly, in bravado. Around a corner a large, solid figure stepped, a darkly unshaven man, disappearing at once into the unlit gloom of a concrete recess.

There were no lighting schemes then. What lighting there was remained unrestored to function. There were no closed-circuit cameras to record the moment. Joaquin stepped out of thick shadows at the base of a twelve-storey block, a tender, dark face, a large, broad, muscular shape. He could have been a murderer.

I recognised him from the people selling radical newspapers on the library steps. He was wearing the same army-surplus jacket I had seen before. His head had been shaved maybe two weeks ago. Now the hair was even all over to a length of a quarter of an inch, showing the first signs of curliness, like astrakhan fur. He had shaved his chin more recently, but not very recently. He came towards us with hand outstretched – I think Joaquin was the first person I knew who shook hands on meeting you. He had carried on shaking hands without any kind of reference to how people greeted each other in the place he now lived. The noise he made as he approached was of slapping – he wore yellow flip-flops with his jeans. He shook my hand, too, with warmth and energy, and with a burst of bright whiteness in his cheerful mouth. From his body came a physical smell, quite strong. It was a fleshy smell, Joaquin's odour, the smell of an animal who has run a good deal, but not at all unpleasant. He was perfectly clean, but never used perfumes or deodorants, either to mask or to erase what his flesh smelt of. 1982 was an age of anti-perspirants and guilt and fretting, deodorants called Worry for Men and a pong of metal and chemicals in the mornings on buses and in classrooms. I think I can honestly say that it was Joaquin's smell – the smell of a warm human body at ease with itself – that changed my mind as much as what I heard people say. I wanted to be in a room with this man.

'Who is this?' Joaquin said politely. 'I know Eric and James and Tracy and Mohammed but this one, no.'

'I'm Spike,' I said.

'We only have tea and maybe not milk,' Joaquin said. 'I come down. I came down for you. Kate told me I must come. She says you don't know where to come. I tell her she must be crazy; you've been a hundred times to our place. Number 712, seventh floor. Elevator is not working. As always not working.'

'How did you know we were coming?' Tracy said.

'I came down and I waited,' Joaquin said. 'I waited for you, Tracy.'

'Oh, fuck off,' Tracy said.

Joaquin gave a brief, joyous bark of laughter. 'No, we see you coming. Don't you know that? On the seventh floor, we see all the way over the city, we see anyone coming over the bridge, you know, the footbridge on the dual carriageway –' this phrase produced with care and some pride, a phrase recently mastered, perhaps '– and tonight we see one-two-three-four-five-six kids coming and Kate she says who is the sixth and Euan says his friend Percy mentioned a new friend comrade and I say good, I go down and meet them, bring them up if Kate says it's necessary. Today six comrades. Tomorrow maybe we see the police and the army running over to us, come to arrest or shoot us, me and Kate and Eu-aron –' it was always touching, the lengths Joaquin went to not to call Euan Juan – 'and I tell you, we see them coming with their batons and guns and uniform, and we know what to do. But today it is again Percy and the good guys we see coming. Ten minutes ago.'

Joaquin burst out laughing once more, there on the second floor ascending the flights of stairs. We didn't have the same right as he did, the survivor (at twelve) of real policemen running over real bridges to take action, the right to laugh at the idea if he chose to. We waited, impressed and disconcerted. It was my first glimpse of Joaquin's lightness of spirit, the way that for him things both mattered and didn't matter, could be done away with and forgotten or fiercely engaged with, given a good slap. It depended not on their inherent gravity but on the dignity and decision of the thinking person. The spirit of laughter. There was nothing in the world like Joaquin's laughter. It came up from the depths of him, in his bowels and belly, a sound that burst out like a single man applauding in a crowded place, and could make strangers turn around and even, sometimes, join in. There was a ripple and a gurgle in it you could never forget. I loved Joaquin's laugh. I still do. Did he think that the English policemen were going to run across the bridge over the dual carriageway to beat him and his flatmates into submission because of their ideological convictions? They could not, while he could laugh at the idea. That was stronger than any policeman. And so Joaquin went out after midnight with lightness in his heart to paint walls and to smash windows. Of course he did.

'Did you come on the bus?' Joaquin asked.

'No,' Mohammed said. 'Ogden drove us. He passed his test last month.'

'He's got his mum's car,' James Frinton said, quite neutrally.

'He's parked it in that multi-storey car park by the library,' Mohammed said. 'He thought it would be safer there.'

This was clearly meant as a jibe, but Joaquin either didn't catch the tone or didn't see the point.

'Yes,' he said. 'Very good idea. Not to come down here and leave it. Not safe. The little kids round here, they strip it, smash the windows, cut the wheels, the tyres. Or I tell you, last week, these kids, they break into a lady's flat, old lady. Two, three flats away from us, she's sitting there, can't do anything, was watching, they take TV in front of her, take it out, throw the TV out of the window, bang, explodes. Why? No idea. I have not the foggiest. You are underneath a TV falling from seventh floor, I tell you, you know about it when it hits you, or even car, empty, bash, bang. No, that's good idea, park your mum's car in the multi-storey. Gonna be safe there.'

I glimpsed the kind of authority that Joaquin had. Nobody contradicted him or reverted to the previous stages of the argument. The only resistance to Joaquin's sensible-sounding point was James Frinton, saying, 'Well, but they're deprived, aren't they, these kids, they're the real victims here.'

'I tell you what these kids are,' Joaquin said. 'They are the total little cunts. Mrs Gunnarsson, she's scared now all day long, and guess what, she has no TV. So the real victims – no. They are the real total little cunts. And here we are at last home. I wish they mend that fucking elevator some time.'

Joaquin jiggled at the blue-painted door. In the pane of glass, there was a small poster advertising a people's gathering with the date of a year earlier. The door stuck, then fell inwards. We all followed Joaquin in, dumping our coats on a plastic chair in the hallway. There were pairs of scuffed shoes, walking boots, old plimsolls and two more pairs of flip-flops, red and green. On the wall was a framed front page of the Spartacist newspaper – I can't now remember what it was called, although I know it wasn't 'The Spartacist'. But I remember that the issue they had gone to the trouble of framing was one they had produced to celebrate the royal wedding a year or two before. Over a photograph of the happy couple in uniform and medals and massive cream finery in taffeta was a headline reading 'GET OUT THE GUILLOTINE'. Underneath, a subhead purported to claim that 2,745 malnourished children in inner cities could have been fed for a year on the cost of that one dress. A brilliant piece of fabrication, I learned later. They had been turned away by three framing shops.

'Hi, honey,' Joaquin called. 'We're home.'

A thin wail of delight came from upstairs – it was, I realised, a two-floor flat, something I didn't know was possible.

'I got the kids,' Joaquin said, trotting upwards, his flat brown hairy feet slapping happily. 'And a new one, too! What's your name?'

A woman came to the door of the sitting room, a wide, untidy blonde woman. Her hair was up and in it, like a Japanese woman's hair-chopsticks, was a pair of biros. She had been writing. Her tools were her ornament, her display. The sitting room behind her had a long, plate-glass window, giving out onto the city centre. From here, it was a long way down to the grime and the empty, dumpy streets smelling of piss and beer. And Joaquin was right. From there you could see anyone approaching across the bridge over the dual carriageway – police thugs, young radicals, anyone. They were up there looking down on the direction that humanity could take, whether individuals or in groups. I was overcome with admiration and envy. I wanted to be these people. Joaquin's physical presence in particular filled me with joy – the teeth, the hair, the wonderful smell of him as he cast off his jacket, dropping it on the floor, his hairy humorous feet idling and gripping the yellow flip-flops, a joy that, at that moment, I did not quite understand. If I'd had an explanation it would soon have been proved incomplete.

Introductions were made. Kate kissed each of us, including me. (But she had only just met me, I remember thinking, with a bourgeois stuffiness about intimacy rituals that I tried to suppress.) 'Welcome, Spike,' Kate said formally. Now it is clear that she was a doctor's daughter, only twenty years old, just as uncertain as any of us, trying to make up her mind how to live and how to improve the lives of people she would never meet, subject like any of us to vulgar complaints like love. She seemed immeasurably wise and experienced, like Goldberry in Tolkien. Her poetry, when I came to read it, was quite wonderful.

> Magic can happen on a bus
> To anyone.
> On the window the mud was like filigree.
> And the man sitting next to me
> On the magical bus
> Which was red
> Said in a stagey way that he was struck with love.
> Like an angel he looked deeply and passionately into my eyes.

She would show me this poem, and twenty or thirty more, in another week's time. Joaquin was beyond anything my experience held, but even Kate was extraordinarily mature and thoughtful and impressive. I was not the only one who felt this. The others had gone silent since Joaquin had met us, walking up the seven flights of stairs in a quiet that could only have been awestruck. They were only four or five years older than us. They were separated from us by the lifespan of a pair of

Y-fronts. But the awe was there, hanging in the air like the smoke-hung echo after an explosion.

We'd just missed Euan. He was out, Kate said, doing whatever he had to be doing – it was early in the evening to be painting on walls, so I guess he was at some meeting or men's group or an ecological action.

'Dressed in a suit,' Joaquin said.

'That's the thing,' Kate said. 'You don't dress to stand out if you've got an action in mind, and with a bit of luck you slide under the radar. The other day – no, last month – Joaquin comes in and he sees me and Euan and I'm wearing a jumper and skirt and pearls, fake pearls from Woolworth's, and Euan's wearing a tweed jacket he found in Oxfam. And you said, didn't you –'

'I said what the hell, Kate,' Joaquin said happily. 'And they are going they tell me to a meeting, to this Fascist group, the Monday Club, is it? At the university. Euan he had a bottle of piss, he throws it at the speaker they got, it smashes, they run. I wish I go there too. But no suit, no jacket, no tie. No me.'

'And I guess they'd remember three people but two – it's just a bloke and his girlfriend,' I said. I surprised myself. 'They won't recognise you if they see you the next day. Different clothes.'

'Yeah, that's it,' Kate said. 'And I brushed my hair. This one gets the point. We like you. You can come again.' She made me think what an unlikely revolutionary she was, an implausible and unsuspected hurler of bottles of piss, an innocuous painter of walls, a smooth-faced smasher of windows. 'Come out with us. Deal with the cunts.'

It was only that last word that made me see Kate as she wanted to be seen. It made me see that she and not Joaquin was the destructive presence there, the presence utterly focused on herself and her own voice and deeds. All her energy was spent presenting herself. Her interest in those around her was a performance, made to cloak her with a sympathetic air. But at first she was not interesting. She was only sympathetic. I reached out to this sympathy. Like most men, I wanted my voice to be heard above all things.

'Bourgeois pacifist,' Joaquin was saying, 'no army, no nuclear weapons, your friends in Campaign Nuclear Disarm, your friends, Percy, you know what I'm saying?'

'They're not my friends,' Percy said. 'I haven't agreed with them for years.'

'Well, you lose the nuclear and you leave the Soviet revolution without defence,' Joaquin said. 'Hey, I tell you what...'

Kate got up. Her attention had been drawn, too. Handling it delicately, she extracted a flyer from a red folder on top of the dusty old TV. It was advertising a CND rally at City Hall the following week. Campaign for Nuclear Disarmament. It's a sign of those long-gone times that an organisation like the CND could, in the early 1980s, command a space holding several thousand people. There was a general feeling of doom and despair, I remember, and quite unexpected people had signed up to the proposal that these weapons should be removed from the Earth through a process of disarmament. It was even a bone of contention between my friends Matthew and Simon, who never thought about politics in my sense. One wanted abolition, the other believing in a balance of awesome forces to maintain a tranquillity of existence. The point of view, like the Spartacists', that believed the most important point was that the Soviets not only had a nuclear arsenal but should use it at some point was, I believe, an unusual one even at the time. It didn't take long for Kate to persuade us that a good thing to do would be to go along to the CND rally the following week and fuck it up. There wouldn't be that much dressing up to do.

'Cunts,' Kate said, of the bourgeois pacifists, her eyes shining.

Somehow I found myself with Joaquin on the flat's small open space, a little enclosed balcony. I don't know how we got there. There was no alcohol along the line. I didn't feel drunk, just open to the possibility of intoxication. Joaquin must have got up in his big, confident way, carrying his mug of tea. Like a duckling, I must have got up too. I would have followed his flapping flip-flops out. I think what it must have looked like. Tracy's bare feet all at once kneading away at the space where I had been sitting. I don't think I gave it a moment's consideration back then in 1982. The world was changing.

'Have you seen the view that we have?' Joaquin said. His dark eyes were full of pleasure. He was being funny. For some reason to do with design, the balcony we stood on faced away from the city and the lights and what money could produce, and towards the steeply rising black hill that had always been there. A spottily inhabited final block intervened. Then darkness.

'You can see everything,' I said, trying to be funny. 'Grass. The other building.'

'It's interesting, you know? The fifth floor up, seven windows from the left – Spike, count, I show you, three, five, seven, okay? – there's an old man. Lives there. Very fat. Sunday afternoon, every Sunday afternoon this happens. He takes off all his clothes, walks round, one hour. Then he puts his clothes back on. Sits down again. I forget the important part, sorry, excuse me. Lives there with big fat old lady too, his wife, I guess. Sunday afternoon she goes out. She puts on hat and coat, goes out, shuts the front door, okay, then it is he takes off all his clothes, walks around, very pleased, very happy, one hour, puts back on, sits down, wife comes home. What the fuck, what, why? Don't know. Can't say. Interesting, I guess. You know?'

'Maybe he just wants to have something that his wife doesn't know anything about. His naked hour once a week.'

33

'I guess,' Joaquin said. Then he brightened. 'Strange thing, though. Everyone knows about it. Just not his wife. We see him every Sunday, know he's gonna do this. Same with everyone in this block. They all know the fat old man naked over there, Sunday two thirty, three thirty. We like it. Kate and Euan and me, Sunday lunch, whole Spartacist family, finish eating, come down and sit here on this balcony and watch the performance. Very, very nice.'

'Does he wank?'

'Does he – excuse me? Does he – oh, no. Nothing like that. Just a big pink fat baby, only that. How old are you, Spike – Spike, yes? I never heard your name before.'

'I'm sixteen,' I said.

'I see,' Joaquin said. 'And you just now start to think about things – is that the fact of things? When you are sixteen you start to think the world, it is not how I want it. How it must be. And one day you say to a man, a friend, a stranger like me, the world it can change and that friend or stranger he says…'

He was lost for a moment. I caught a whiff again of Joaquin's smell – rich, toffee-like, a sour metallic edge to it. He bared his teeth at me, a grin in the dark.

'What's Chile like?' I said boldly.

'Oh, you have discovered it,' Joaquin said. 'My English is not good because I was in England for ten years even. You have to know – my mother she kept us at home for three years after we came. They only found out I was there and must go to school when I was fourteen and then I spoke English for the first time. So, yes. I am Chilean and my English is not good.'

'I didn't mean that,' I said. 'I honestly only meant to ask what Chile is like.'

'Okay, I don't understand,' Joaquin said. 'But they told you about me, I see! So Chile, it is a shithole now. There is no future there, it's all gone. My father he had friends, and now they are in Canada or Australia, Spain, maybe one in Nicaragua.

Another shithole. Portugal, here in England. I don't know where they all go in the end. When I am a kid, they meet every week, twice a week, your house, my house, his house. Ten-minute walk from where you are living, two minutes in the car, or you ask your driver to stay where he is and finish his dinner, you are happy to walk. That kind of life. But now they are never going to see each other ever again. Those are the lucky ones.'

'What do you mean?' I said.

'The lucky ones are still alive, you know. My father was not so lucky. He is buried – his body is buried, excuse me – behind a police station somewhere. I guess. Maybe most of his body, not all the finger bones. They cut those off earlier. The usual story. He must have suffered before he died. My mother, she brings us to England.

'That was strange to me. The only time I go out of Chile before that was when I was eight. My father he is invited to East Germany. He is a hero of the German Democratic Republic and they ask him to come and bring his family, two weeks' holiday and an award for international friendship. I remember that very well. And then we are in England, everything very strange, with my mother in this house in London. All the time she is saying that he escaped, he is fine, he is in Guatemala or in the - I don't know - Seychelles maybe. She thinks he doesn't phone us because then, ring-ring, the Chilean government guys they are listening in and then they know where to find him. I have a sister. To her, too, she says that when we are safe your father comes and finds us. I don't know that she believes what she says. She says that all the time we are in the flat, three years, just us in London, Camden Town - you know Camden Town?'

'I'm sorry,' I said.

'Oh, sorry? Sorry is still to come,' Joaquin said. He was quite calm, even with the appearance of enjoyment. He was fixing me with a look of real concentration. From inside the flat came a yell of disappointment – I think it was Percy Ogden, groaning over some false or implausible move in an argument. He hated to lose an argument, and he pretended to hate an inadequate challenge in argument. Joaquin must have heard this sound many times before, probably more often than I had. He went on with his own familiar story. 'What happened, okay, is that a guy comes one day to our house in Camden Town. I know this guy, I see his face from the old days, and he comes in and sits with my mother for two hours. Me I get told, go away, take your sister Rosa, nothing to hear. Then he goes. What I think now is that this guy he shows my mother something, tells her something that afterwards she doesn't think – no, she knows that there is no husband in Guatemala or Seychelles. Hiding until the time is safe. Then she understands, no question, he is no longer living, not writing because he is beyond all that. So the little family goes on. It has to. I don't know how my mother goes on. I guess if you have son, twelve, thirteen, and little girl too, then you have to, you must go on. So there it is. What happened to you?'

Joaquin's tone was guileless, apparently a real question. It was what people said when they noticed that a stranger had injured his face, for example, or torn his clothes, nothing more than that. In a moment I understood what he meant, perhaps enquiring about what series of injustices had set me off on the radical path, to be standing with a South American revolutionary on a balcony so small that, if either of us moved, our bodies briefly brushed against each other. But there was no injustice. The injustices were yet to come. Everything had been comfort, indulgence, opportunity, and the usual comment of the sixteen-year-old that none of this was fair. It wasn't fair, but that, I felt, would not keep me on the balcony with Joaquin. I said something absurd. It had worked before.

'I read *Das Kapital*,' I said.

'No,' Joaquin said, with amusement. 'No, you didn't read the *Capital*. It doesn't matter, but you don't need to say that. You like those others? You like the boy James, James Frinton?'

'Well, yes,' I said, surprised, adding lamely, 'He lives in a pub.' That was the most interesting thing about him.

'He's a strange one,' Joaquin said. 'I don't know why it's him who's the leader of that group you're in.'

I looked at him, amazed. 'He's not the leader,' I said. Then I remembered the world as it should be. I said, 'The group doesn't have leaders. How should it?' But of course I had been surprised, not because Joaquin had thought the group had a leader but because he had identified the wrong one. Ogden was the leader, the guiding political spirit.

'He listens to everything,' Joaquin said. 'Then maybe he says something. Everyone likes him. I guess I like him. His mother, you've met the mother? Kate says she's crazy, the father bastard only interested in money but can't make money. He's on his own, he knows that. Kate goes to see him once, just wants to see. What makes this guy? I tell you. If I am sixteen and woman, twenty, comes to see me, my mother very concerned about it. Those parents they don't care. He's on his own. He's going to make his life his self. It's like he's an orphan and, believe me, an orphan sixteen years old, that's a dangerous thing. Like me, an orphan. We say whatever we need to say.'

'Would you ever go back to Chile?' I said. I could see Joaquin at the head of an army of widows, orphans, exiles, revolutionaries, standing in a hurtling jeep in the hot sun, hurtling under arches of white bougainvillaea and hibiscus, his arms outspread in acknowledgement and welcome.

'Chile, no,' Joaquin said, bright with hilarity. 'That is over for me. Someone else can deal with it. Put it right. What I have to do is here and now. You know what I mean?'

What astonished me was to discover that Joaquin and I were exactly the same height. He had seemed so big, and so physically substantial with bone and hard flesh. I hardly knew how to place myself in relation to that physical scale. It was only now that I discovered our faces were in the same place, exactly level, six feet above the concrete floor of the balcony where marigolds, scarlet geraniums, marijuana plants, purple, pink, aquamarine and yellow snapdragons sat in pots, one warm evening, within the all-including rich, masculine smell of Joaquin, the revolutionary. Joaquin's kiss, when it came, was a fact of inevitable nature, like a warm front predicted on the news bulletin and then experienced without surprise, recognised rather, a fact quite external to our characters. I had no idea, or not much, that it was in me to kiss a twenty-two–year-old Chilean Spartacist until it was actually happening, and once it started, I had a moment of shock, almost alarm, that I am a male and I am being kissed by another male before a more certain and individual sense that I was meant to be kissed like this, with the solid arms around my back and shoulders, the thick trunk of the tongue in my mouth, pushing back at my own tongue, the rough rub of Joaquin's face against mine and, I knew, my right hand gripping the short curly hair on the flat back of Joaquin's head. His odour was all around me. I closed my eyes and was within it. I had kissed girls before, but I had never, it now seemed, been kissed. Everything in the world that was soft and tentative, pink, blushing and yielding was gone from my life in a moment. I had no idea where I found myself in this new world of definite statements and solid certainty. I had no idea where I was. From now on I resolved to devote my life to the liberation of the urban proletariat.

Joaquin pulled back for a moment, his arms still around me. His beautiful face was filled with laughter and amused joy.

'The way you were looking at me,' he said, and he plunged once more at my face.

Born on Sunday, Silent

Désirée Reynolds

I FELL IN LOVE with myself from early on. I fell in love with my name. I knew I couldn't stay put, but so hated to miss anything I decided to come back, over and over, until something was revealed to me. Because come back is what we do. I went on a journey to find someone like me, but I only found versions of me that were disconnected from other versions of me. The trees were heavy with leaves, they touched each other and I felt their caress. The grass a pillow and the stone a bed. Remember. Born on Sunday. Kai Akosua Mansah. Do not forget it or get it wrong. It tires me, this casual wrongness, this no need for correction. My father was not a chief or a warrior but the man that was tasked to dig ditches. We were neither noble nor savage. We dug ditches. Ditches that were straight, ditches that curled around forests or followed the path of the moon. I was born on a Sunday, the third female child to my mother. Not yet moving and moving all the time. Born on Sunday. Empire delivers a cold breath that twists the trees. The trees please me here. Kai Akosua Mansah. Born on Sunday, silent.

I cross roads, I jump water, I climb trees, I walk the paths. I went to the house of learning a long time ago. I wanted to find myself and myself wanted to feel not so alone. Small fists gripping myself. Small. Small fists. I am Kai Akosua. Like the last point of an echo, getting smaller and quieter as time goes, that the noise is forgotten, edited, it is done. My bed. Open to wind. I saw floods, that came from the hills to wash away the rest of the people not killed by war or sickness. Died sleeping. The clocks did not stop for me. The mirrors kept their shine. And so that we don't continuously come to you, flung up by water and body snatchers, we were put here. But I venture. The others were still and restful, whereas I liked to walk 'abroad'. A funny way to say be about. Take in the things around me. Observe and listen. But not learning. I had already done a lot of that.

'A man of learning eloquence and piety.'
　　The trees droop, bent under death, with branches that arch over William Gilbert. With palm trees and a globe, to depict the places he took for his own. When to explore might have meant to lose. To lose yourself in other than home. Bright red roofs where trees once were, I can see the land is shrinking. On the steps of the chapel. I'm home and not home. Home is in your eyes and mine, but I am eyeless. Kai. Third daughter. Daughter. The stone feels cold under me, hard and smooth and shaped. The only edges are on the grave stones that stand like empty houses. Eternal rest. Eternal sleep. Born sleeping. I was born sleeping and to sleep I will back to. I am Kai.
　　I tried to find some others. In a city as old as Sheffield there must be others. More like me, far from home but here to stay. We are all silent here but some more than others. Except Samuel. Samuel Morgan Smith curled his American tongue around the words he spat out every March. He stands upon Mark Firth – who does not like it one bit – and becomes what he calls The Noble Moor. He rants. His noise rattles down the mossy sides and to the gates where it launches out. So concerned is he with his performance that he doesn't see me. Fool. Show off. He was here when I got here, and I believe

him to be more lost than I. He tells to me of not home. We are both not home.

I left my bed, others still holding on and I went out of the grand gate, crossed Stalker Lees Road and went to the place of learning down the street because I thought it would teach me a way to get back home, but I was trapped here. Among the demands of weed and food and attention and sometimes sex. Trapped in an idea of me that they were more interested in than I. Every day other requests came. Not to ask about me or what I was doing or feeling, but about my hair, my skin, my food and if I didn't have any weed could I find someone that did. It was like being in the fake village all over again.[1]

I started to feel like a disappointment. Being eager to please, it sometimes hurt when I couldn't. The white dreds never smiled in my direction. My blackness made me black and at the same time invisible. I walked the lawns at Collegiate Crescent. It seemed to be that this house of learning contained idiots and fools and no one who could tell me about home. Third daughter. What of my sisters? What of one and two? As if I, a child, can understand that connection that made me, as if a child, born on Sunday, silent, is knowing of any other desire but for my mother, my home, my breath. Home is a lost sentence, a foreign land I have no visa for. I sat in the room and listened to the different accents and opinions and people talking over me and around me but they wanted me to laugh at unfunny jokes about myself. Performing a kind of fat blackness that was comfortable for all, unchallenging and open. This is the blackness you wanted, not the small fists gripping nothing or the cries for home or the ditch digger.

'I don't see why we have to talk about race all the time, it's not necessary in every situation.'

People in the seminar, which is in a room in a house that looks like I might have lived in the attic or the basement, murmur and nod. The woman from Madras who is trying to

41

get them to see us, using more breath than is needed, I watch the curls fall over her bindi.

'That is, essentially, what someone who isn't impacted by the issues and complexities of race might say.'

She spoke with patience, housing each word with her breath and the roof of her mouth.

Silence is always what hangs in the air, she absorbs the violence of us being contested. I do not absorb. I reflect. The mirrors are left uncovered. The clocks haven't stopped.

The war that brought us under the English boot also took us here. A broken warrior should not be displayed. But such a price for food or freedom. Ditch diggers can dance. But I can't. Born on Sunday. There is our gold that hangs from your ears, necks and wrists. Four hundred years of looting and yet my fists are empty. But the silence contains a brutality. An unknowing that witnesses nothing. Not cries for home, noises of death and solitude, misused and broken bodies, lost babies, three or four in one family and lost families, homes with rats, that nibble at you when you're sleeping, with the sounds of empty bellies and clinking glasses.

When I came here in my mother's belly, you had already been there lifetimes. As she squatted against the cold, in so much cloth she could barely move. She and her sisters and my sisters, crouching over pots and their weaving. They watch the ditch digger dance. I tell her I'm here. I tell her I'm coming.

I walked about the graves in daylight, the sun sometimes lost in the trees. My story was lost to me. I carried my bag and books and sat on the temple steps, looking over at the grandeur of the headstones of the rich and powerful living to old ages, but where I sleep, with so many others, was poor. The poor have no names. I am the only one here that does. They beg to borrow it sometimes, I always say no. Kai Akosua is mine. There are graves that have two wives in it. How do they get along?

When I went to the Central Library, the people there looked me in the eye and told me I didn't exist. Empire and the slave trade rested differently, they had untethered them from each other. They gave me a big folder. I pointed out that there are only notes on abolition. Wilberforce, Mary Anne Rawson.

'But where is the information about Sheffield and the slave trade?'

'We don't like talking about that. It's too uncomfortable.'

I liked that she hadn't pretended that it didn't matter. I liked that she looked at me.

The librarian shook her head, with a disbelief and embarrassment she said: 'We don't want to hear about what we did, only what we did about it.' She looked out at the full shelves of books, as if still looking for the answers.

'This is not accidental,' I tell her.

'No,' she says, 'we just don't do it. And yet, to have this folder about abolition seems to tell us what the focus was. There would not have been a strong abolitionist movement here if there wasn't the effects or ramifications of the slave trade and slavery too.'

The other librarian agreed and I thanked them.

'Have you tried the archive?'

Looking for Sheffield past was not easy, the things that get left out tell a story all of their own.

Poking around old things is what I like to do. I think I will be sat in a room with letters and boxes and dusty declarations of love or hate or greed. I am not though. The woman shows me to a c-o-m-p-u-t-e-r. The answers are only as good as the questions that I ask it. Meetings to discuss abolition reported in newspapers, chartists and again Mary Anne.

How can books contain so much silence? How can this c-o-m-p-u-t-e-r?

I see her still. Thinking over c-u-p-s-o-f-t-e-a and wondering to herself.

On the steps I wrote insignificant things. Maybe there was no story. The shadow cast over my pages was a man, a drunk, who had made it his job to talk to everyone. But every black person knows that talking to someone new is a gamble. What are they going to say? When does the violence start?

William Parker sold planters their knives and forks. Because eating with their blood-soaked hands would be frowned upon around the table.

And yet I'm prepared now, as you listen or not listen to me. The silence is not accidental, but wilful and spiteful. Will you honour it this time?

Paul Eagle Star dies in this city. In the papers, I saw on the computer, he is described as being 'best behaved' among the braves. He was best behaved and I, the third daughter of a ditch digger. He is softly spoken, he has the sad eyes of his horse, mourns the children he did not get to raise. When he walks, I cannot hear him. He says he is glad he's home. And wishes the same for me.

I am born on Sunday, silent. I walk the paths. I roll down the steep banks. I jump water. I climb trees. Home is a memory that I don't have. And all I remember is here. Be that as it may, it is only left to say, with my hand on chest where there is no heartbeat, that you move along now. You have taken too much already.

Note

1. The Ashanti Village – over 100 Africans were brought over to Sheffield for entertainment in December 1902. Kai Akosua Mansah, an Ashanti baby, is buried in a common grave in Sheffield General Cemetery. Born 1902. Died in infancy 1902.

The Father Figure

Geoff Nicholson

IT HAPPENED AGAIN. This time when I was in the Sheffield Botanical Gardens, a place I'd been going to most of my life, a place I used to go when I was skiving off school. Yeah, I was a proper little rebel. I was sitting on a bench in front of the grand glass houses, pavilions if we're being precise, the sun had faded, the day had turned cold, and I was thinking I might get up and take another walk around the bear pit, when I saw my father, a man who had been dead for fifteen years.

Well, of course, I didn't think it really was my father. I didn't believe it was a ghost or a visitation, but neither did I think it was a projection from my own imagination. I didn't know what it was, what I was seeing, and I'd got to the point where I didn't expect to find out.

In front of me, walking along the path between the herbaceous, was a man, clearly a real, flesh-and-blood human being. He was not in any way extraordinary except that he looked exactly the way my father had in his later years, when he was healthy, before he had the illness that killed him. This man had the same build, the same way of carrying himself, the same slightly faded grey and light brown clothes. He looked fine. He looked very much alive.

The only thing that was 'wrong,' the only thing that wasn't like my father: this old guy was walking a dog, a large bundle of shaggy, tired energy. My father had never owned a dog, and had never allowed me to have one: too much trouble, too much responsibility. These days I tend to think he had a point.

I was no longer surprised by this kind of sighting, no longer alarmed, nor frightened, nor even all that curious. It had happened too often, and I'd been living with it too long. The very first time it happened was at my dad's funeral.

It was one of the few I've attended, and one of only two I've ever organised, the other being my mum's, but the 'organisation' didn't extend much beyond calling the Co-op Funeral Service, picking a price, and leaving the rest to them.

My dad and I had never discussed funeral arrangements, we'd rarely talked about anything serious at all, but I do remember something he said while he was sitting in the brown velour armchair in the living room of the semi in Gleadless where my parents lived, a spot to which he grew ever more attached as the illness took hold. He looked up from his crossword and said, 'I have my doubts about life after death. But then I'm not even all that convinced about life before death.'

It was the kind of thing he'd often say, not quite a joke, not quite serious, not exactly profound, but more than just small talk. I smiled and let it go. I hadn't been able to come up with a snappy reply.

He died quickly. He had severe back pain which turned out to be a symptom of renal cancer, but this is not a story about the horrors of cancer, I'm sure you know as much about them as you need to.

I imagined there might be a Rolls Royce hearse at the funeral, to carry the coffin to the City Road Crematorium. I knew my dad had never travelled in a Rolls, and I did think it would be a sad thing if the only time he ever rode in one was on the way to his own cremation. But when the hearse turned up it was just a Daimler. I didn't know if that was better or worse.

As we turned into the driveway of the crematorium, I looked out of the car window, and standing there by the entrance gate was a man who looked uncannily, unsettlingly like my dad. Of course I thought it was strange and I didn't know what to make of it, but I had a lot of other things on my mind at that moment. I had a part to play at the funeral. I didn't want to break character.

But when the business was over, as we stood about outside making awkward, heavy conversation, I thought again about Dad's double, and I looked around trying to see him again. There was no sign of him, and I admit I was relieved. By then I had also started to construct a convincing explanation. Obviously it wasn't my dad, just somebody who looked like him, maybe a friend from work. And I told myself it wasn't really so very surprising. Men of a certain age and type tend to have friends who look much the same way that they do. I didn't for a moment think it was in any sense him, not a spectre or a spirit. It was just one of those bizarre experiences, coincidence, synchronicity, weird stuff that happens. I didn't tell anybody what I'd seen, certainly not my mum, and not even my wife, now my ex-wife.

The next sighting came in Weston Park. In a way that was not so surprising. My dad died in the Weston Park Hospital, and Weston Park was a place he'd taken me once in a while when I was a kid; to the museum with its stuffed polar bear, the transparent beehive, the drawers full of bugs mounted on pins. I was there in the park again about two months after he died. It was a sentimental journey, I suppose, but I wasn't trying to make a drama out of it, I just wanted to sit quietly. But drama followed me, and again I saw a man who looked just like my dad. This one was trotting down the steps of the

Mappin Art Gallery, moving quickly, and then he strode off at a good clip towards the park gates. I was about fifty yards away and if I'd been determined, I might have been able to catch up and say something to him. But I didn't try. There seemed no pressing reason. Somehow I already knew this was going to be one of many.

Over the years there have been, on average, maybe two sightings a year. That may not seem very many but over a decade and a half it adds up. They were all in and around Sheffield – (I never had a sighting when I went away on holiday) – at Meadowhall, at Midland Station, once in the crowd at Hillsborough though my dad was never a Wednesday fan, in the Peace Gardens, once on a hiking trail by Castleton, once in a taxi line in Barker's Pool, once in a crowded pub in Grenoside, once buying wood in B&Q. The events soon ceased to be especially intense or poignant. They simply became part of my life. One place he didn't show up was at my mum's funeral, and you know, something told me he wouldn't. It would have been too obvious, too neat.

I never tried to talk to these doppelgängers, though in many cases I easily could have. Partly it was that I didn't want to embarrass myself or anyone else. Going up to a stranger and saying, 'Hey you look just like my dead dad,' is asking for trouble. What are they supposed to do with that bit of information? What can they say in return?

There was another reason too, and I know this may sound a bit flakey, but I feared that if I did make contact with any of these sightings, if I spoke to them, if I even took a surreptitious picture with my phone, that would somehow break the spell, that would be the end of things, and I might never see my dad again. I wasn't quite ready for that.

Now, in the Botanical Gardens, the man with the dog approached, got nearer, came very close, and then, to my surprise and discomfort, sat down at the far end of the bench, and the dog stretched himself out on the ground between us.

This was as close as I'd ever been to one of my father's lookalikes. I had expected that when he got really close I'd realise that maybe he didn't look like my dad after all, but no, the resemblance remained convincingly exact. I was close enough to touch him if I wanted to, though I can't say I wanted to, and I was definitely close enough to speak, and despite my fears of breaking the spell, I found myself saying, quietly, calmly, boringly, 'That's a good old dog.'

The man turned to me unsmiling and said, 'Well, he's old anyway.'

That actually sounded like something my dad might have said, and although the voice wasn't exactly like my dad's, it wasn't far off.

For a while I thought that was as much as either of us was going to say, but then the old man said, 'I know you, don't I?'

'Do you?'

'Yes. And you know me.'

He sounded serious and not altogether friendly. I felt my heart beating a little faster. Was he going to say I reminded him of his son, maybe of his dead son? No, he wasn't.

He said, 'You used to go out with my daughter.'

The tone of his voice didn't sound as though it had been a happy affair.

'No,' I said. 'I don't think so.'

I hadn't met the father of every single woman I'd ever dated but it seemed like a very long arm of coincidence that I'd date someone whose father looked exactly like my own.

'I really don't think so,' I said again, trying not to sound too dogmatic. But my new companion was dogmatic enough for both of us.

'Yes, you did,' he said. 'Yes, you fucking did.'

I'd never heard my dad use the f-word, though I assumed he used it regularly outside the house.

'What was her name?' I asked innocently enough, though I knew he wasn't going to like that question.

'You know what her name was.'

I didn't, of course. I waited. I knew he'd say her name.

'Chelsea,' he said.

'No, I never dated anybody named Chelsea. I've never even met anybody called Chelsea.'

'You would say that.'

'Why would I say it if it wasn't true?'

He paused to take a deep breath.

'Because you're a lying little shit and a coward, and because you dumped her and she killed herself, and it was all your fault, you bastard.'

I had heard my dad use the word bastard.

'I'm really sorry to hear about your daughter,' I said, 'but…'

'Sorry? I'll make you sorry.'

The dog at our feet stirred, only slightly it seemed. It didn't adopt an attack pose, didn't yelp or bark or even move more than a few inches, and then with great precision it sank its teeth into my left ankle.

I definitely yelped, and very possibly barked, with the pain. I wanted to say something to the dog owner, in the kind of language I'd never heard my dad use, but the words didn't come. I took off my shoe and my sock and examined the bite. There were four rough, asymmetrical canine incisions around my ankle. They'd pierced the skin, and I was bleeding a little, though I wasn't going to die from it. I rubbed the flesh, dabbed away the blood, and by the time I looked up, man and dog were on their feet and shambling away. As ever, I could have pursued them but, as ever, I didn't.

I was left in a state of confusion, though there was nothing new about that. Had I really resembled the young man who'd once dated his daughter? Had she really killed herself? Had he even had a daughter? Was any of his story true? I had no way of knowing and no way of investigating. I wanted to think he was of no importance, just another nutter in the park, but as time went by that wasn't quite possible.

It turned out I was right about breaking the spell. Since that encounter in the Botanical Gardens with the man and his dog, I haven't had another sighting of my dad. I really do miss him. But then I always did.

How to Love What Dies

Gregory Norminton

EVERY NATION HAS ITS ghosts, but few are as attached to their
ghosts as the English. I learned this as a reader long before we
came here. Perhaps the fog is to blame (not that fog is
common, these days), or the darkness that scarcely lifts an
eyelid in the short days of winter. For ghosts need the dark to
reveal them. They are vapour, like water, and neither the Tigris
nor the Euphrates are enough to summon them, only the
ancient damp of English clay.

   This is, perhaps, the story of a haunting. It would not
make the anthologies of ghost stories that I used to read: it is
too irresolute and refutable. If the hairs stand up on the back
of your neck, it is because what happens in the *living* world
still has power to shock you, or you have not yet lost your
power to be shocked. I am writing not because I truly expect
anyone to read this, but because, an elderly widower, I have no
one with whom to share what has happened.

★

I came twenty years ago to this country, with my wife and our
son, when civil war engulfed our homeland. The government
settled us in Sheffield, far from the England I had encountered
in books. We were nervous; we slept badly; our boy had

53

nightmares. But we met with much kindness. There is less of that today. Refugees win elections for those who oppose them, though in opposing them they do all they can to hasten that tide of need. I cannot pretend that the new government does not frighten me. Its rhetoric is worse, for now, than its actions, but it is in the nature of such rhetoric that it must be enacted eventually, and with increasing zeal.

My son drew this conclusion two years ago. He lives in Scotland now. But I am not yet ready to despair of my adopted country. Do we owe a debt to our sanctuary even when its nature changes? For I have friends in Sheffield, networks of sympathy from which I cannot easily detach myself.

We met, on our arrival in this city, with many instances of hospitality, not least from the local authority, which in a sense owed my family and me nothing. We were given a small house in Pitsmoor, not far from the cemetery. While we waited for settled status, our son was welcomed at the local primary. We had very little money, but we were kept from hunger and the only real deprivation that I suffered was a creative one. For in my native land I had been a poet of a little renown. By vocation, that is; of necessity, and by family tradition, I was a shopkeeper, a seller of souvenirs of the ruins of an ancient city. Ruins, alas, had been too durable for the men in black, who reduced them to rubble, and where possible to dust (and even that they would have destroyed – the ancient, historical dust that put their moment into context – had it only been possible). They have rebuilt the ruins now, a simulacrum, and I wonder if my shop is open, if someone, very like me, is selling replicas of the replicas. Does that shopkeeper stand, as I stood, in the cool of the evening, looking out across the desert? Is it even possible that he spends hours in the quiet season in his office at the back of the shop, reading the plays of William Shakespeare and attempting to write some poetry of his own? Perhaps because I am old and have endured crueller losses since, I am able to contemplate these possibilities without suffering too greatly. The pain is companionable, almost, to one who is without his companion. Back then, however, it burned my heart to think of what we had lost.

To stamp down the grief that threatened to consume me, I walked miles each day, that first summer, into the centre of town sometimes but more often westwards, into the hills. From Pitsmoor to Walkley – the peaceable crowding of its terraced houses like sparrow nests pressed up together. All those shared walls, people overhearing one another's loves and arguments. The first times, accustomed to dread, I feared that I would meet a police roadblock, or the random hostility of strange men. Of course, I went unhindered. I looked not unlike some of the locals. Wandering further, faces became whiter, gardens appeared, the houses took up elbow-room. This was where the bosses had lived, far from the smoke and the drop-hammer's heartbeat. I was not accustomed to such greenery, and came to relish the whispering under-sky of trees, many of which wore ribbons tied there by residents; for the street trees were targets, in their own way, of an ideology. I read the notices and felt indignant for those beings that awaited their senseless martyrdom. I thought of the pillars and temples – forests in stone, as some consider them – that were falling in my own country. I tried to console myself with the sight of mature gardens behind their gritstone walls. (I was to read all that I could lay my hands on, in the Central Library, about the human and natural history of Sheffield, believing that it is possible, with effort, to become a native of a place in which you were not born.) My feet hurt in my city shoes, but I overruled their complaints and wandered further still, through suburbs into farmland, and up to the shaggy expanse of the moors: soft, quiet cousin to my native scrub. Then home, making a fuel of my hunger, along the wooded river valleys – the fairy tale of the Rivelin, where I would tell my son European stories of orphans and wolves and gingerbread cottages, and where trees have almost but not completely exorcised the ghosts of industry; and the green tunnel of the Porter Brook that opens out to millponds and families and a crowded café.

My wife had been reluctant, at first, to join me on these expeditions. When our son was at school, she spent her time online, attempting to communicate with relatives back home, or trying to learn English, so that she would not be mistaken (in her own words) for one of those women who hides behind her husband, frightened by the underdressed natives and the incomprehensible jargon of officialdom. Gradually, however, I coaxed her out, until we walked in all weathers, among allotments and fields, out into the heather, or around the reservoirs; graduating, via irregular buses, to the villages in the hills, to the edges that ice had carved, aeons ago, into the land, to the oak cloughs and the ash woods dying of blight (for even in Arcadia, Death is present). Once, with our son, we made it as far as the village where, centuries ago, people with the plague had sealed themselves away to save their neighbours.

I have thought a great deal about Eyam, over the years. That, among the martyrdoms, uncommonly merits the name. We walked from one house to another, trying to imagine what it had been like, that plague year; the trees in leaf, the cows, unmilked in the meadows, lowing in pain, the weeds reaching through the corn. History, we learned from the plaques and notices, matters to the English. Preserving it is a duty. Yet I see now that England is haunted, in its dotage, by what has been, by what it was and what it thinks it ought to be. Not all ghosts are benign. Some will lead the living to perdition.

In time, our application for settlement was accepted. I found work that my wife considered beneath me – stacking shelves in the local Co-op – but to which I could find no objection, for I was glad to be alive and safe with my small family. (We tried for several years to expand it, but my wife never again conceived, as if something had failed inside her, a vital force been left behind in the rubble of our former home.) My colleagues at the supermarket teased me for my turn-of-phrase, for mine was a bookish English, not a living one; so I set about learning their speech. *Morning, duck,* the manageress said when I clocked in, and *Ta-ra,* I replied when I left in the evening. I learned that there were two options in life, *the Owls* or *the Blades,* and if anybody ever asked (they did not), I would have told them *the Owls,* because blades I had seen at work in ways that my colleagues could not have imagined. How I played with my new words! *Much Ado About Nothing,* my favourite of the comedies, I called now, to no one's amusement but my own, *A Great Owt About Nowt.* When, as often happened in our new flat in Walkley, my family felt the cold, it pleased me to announce that we were *nesh,* that it made our son *mardy,* and our son, the only Sheffielder in the household, informed me that nobody spoke like this now, at least nobody who counted, who was young. No matter: I learned from my colleagues and neighbours, from the people who sold me things and the people to whom I did the selling, that the English make a host of assumptions about each other from their accents, and that some accents have prestige while others do not. I delight in them all, often prolonging a conversation with a stranger just to hear their inflections.

Happiness, after all that we had suffered, was beyond us, but we knew joy and periods close to contentment. Even as Britain began to show morbid political symptoms, even as the weather abandoned all moderation, we felt safe. Sheffield was a gentle city under its rough exterior. Divided, yes, but held together by the centrifugal force of its symbols and stories. People addressed one another in the street, on the buses and trams. They knew what it was to be abandoned by power, to be disposable to the powerful (but power knew this and was beginning to turn resentment to its advantage). My wife and my son and I watched the news every evening. We knew the signs. But how could this overgrown village lose its hospitable heart?

Our son turned against it first, though he claimed it had turned against him, and us, and everyone like us pouring north in hope of shelter or sanctuary. I have visited him in the young republic. He engineers wind turbines in Aberdeen. I am proud of him, and ashamed of myself that I failed to raise a son who was immune to hatred. Perhaps my wife's illness drove him away. When the diagnosis came, he seemed – absurdly, given the free healthcare she received – to blame the country for it. When she succumbed, something broke in my son. Whatever had tethered him to Sheffield and England came loose, and he emigrated.

Today I am a widower, still writing poems that only a few of my fellow refugees read. I work two days a week in an organic food shop in Crookes, walking back down the hill in the evening to our flat, one half of a terraced house that has been, in the past decade, divided by a landlord keen to exploit the housing crisis. I am lucky, living alone, to have three rooms. I no longer know my neighbours. Upstairs, I believed, no one was in residence.

★

The first sounds of occupancy crept into my sleep. I heard running water, it seeped into my dream, and I awoke convinced that there were people upstairs trying so hard to move about stealthily that they gave themselves away. Timbers creaked; a couple of minutes later, a piece of furniture coughed as it was moved across bare floorboards. I sat up and listened. A car horn outside, an ambulance wailing its way to the Northern General. Nothing more. Perhaps the new occupants, having taken possession in the dead of night, had collapsed onto unmade beds, leaving their boxes and opened suitcases washed up around them. I would find out soon enough. Soon enough, I would no longer be alone in the house.

I had work the next day, and stocktaking kept my mind occupied, so that I had quite forgotten about the strangers upstairs by the time I shut my front door. I microwaved some soup, toasted flatbread, and chewed vacantly while watching television. When the news came on, I turned it off and sat in tremulous silence: the blood in my ears perhaps, or the echo of the pictures that I had seen alongside the headlines. I told my wife about my day as I prepared for sleep and pulled back the cover on our bed. Still now I sleep only on my side. I felt reluctant to get into the cold sheets. She told me to rest my head.

Again I was woken by noises upstairs. It was no dream. Someone was pacing so loudly that my dark-swimming eyes could follow them on the ceiling. Now they were directly above me, now they paced into the kitchen, in and out of the bathroom. There followed a couple of dull thuds, then more pacing. I considered putting on my dressing-gown and knocking on the door (they were awake – why should I not?) to introduce myself, to make my reality felt so that they might think to pace a little more softly. I wanted, also, to satisfy my curiosity. It feels wrong to live metres from my fellow humans and not to know their names and faces. However, the pacing stopped, and I felt a physical reluctance to move. Night weakens our defences: it was more than reluctance, it was dread.

Sleep drowned my senses, and in the morning all was quiet. I rose, washed, prayed, and travelled into town. It pleases me some days to sit in the Winter Garden, among the ferns and palms and children exploring. I enjoy the loose, anonymous company of my fellow citizens. After a sandwich for lunch, I spent an hour at the library, dozing in an armchair designed to keep me awake. Later, at the bus-stop, I waited with Charles Dickens for distraction. In the old days, I might have read Mahfouz or Qabbani, but I now know better than to read a book in Arabic in public. Probably the fact of reading any book singles me out. Everybody walks with their heads bowed, stroking their phones. My son says that the internet has broken the world, that it has made people as sociopathic as the whiz kids of Silicon Valley. Had it not been the men in black who turned the web into a recruiting zone? And today, does not every demagogue and populist use it to control the masses? People will burn their own homes to stay at home in the lie that defines them. Symbols of the past, ecumenical kindness, all must be destroyed. For it is hard to kill when you love life; it is hard to mete out injustice when justice is what you thirst for. I have always feared the recklessness of those that despair. It is easy to fight when you love only death.

I was being watched. It was the bus driver, a large man with sweat patches along his collar. Was I getting on?

I boarded and apologised. My wife scolded me for behaving like an old man, and for my self-indulgent sorrow.

Standing outside the house, I looked and saw no lights in the upstairs flat. The naked window reflected the evening sky. There seemed to be nobody home. Nonetheless, I climbed the stairs to introduce myself.

My knuckles refused to knock; they hovered a few inches from the door, and I told myself that I was becoming a recluse, succumbing to the solipsism of the culture.

It was exactly midnight (I know because my eyes opened onto the alarm clock) when I heard the door to the upstairs flat open and close. There were footsteps, then heavy things were dragged across the floor and I thought, absurdly, of bodies in black bags. Fully awake and emboldened by frustration, I stepped out to the lobby at the very moment the upstairs door opened again.

There is a single, dull light above the stairs that casts an aquatic gloom over everything. It is a light that undermines rather than illuminates, washing the face of colour and vitality. The man was in his fifties, at a guess, balding, his face unshaven. Seeing me, he froze in the midst of descending the stairs, one leg forward and the other not daring to join it from the higher step. His gloved hands (but it was not so cold) gripped the stair-rail on one side and pressed against the wall on the other. I doubt he meant to look as surreptitious as he did. For my part, I did not mean to look hostile or distrustful. Still, I knew he was not my landlord – a fat asthmatic Yorkshireman who looks at me, if ever I ask him for help, as if I were asking him to estimate the distance, in metres, to the moon.

'Hello,' I said.

'Hello.'

'Do you –? Is this your home?'

'Yes.'

'You are very welcome!' I told him my name, but he did not reciprocate. His accent sounded familiar. I ventured a couple of words in Arabic. *Please forgive me if I startled you.* He appeared not to understand, for he said nothing, merely gathered his limbs, consolidating his stand.

'I live downstairs,' I said in English. 'I will be your neighbour.'

The man looked at me with a studied blankness and folded his arms across his chest.

'I don't mean to pry,' I said, wanting to be back in my burrow. I retreated, and as I shut the door to my flat – as quietly as I could and as fast as I dared – I heard him conquer the last steps and escape into the street.

It troubled me that I had revealed myself, that I had put

the face of a weak and vulnerable old man on the abstraction of the downstairs flat. Feelings I had hoped never to meet again welled up inside me. The man was not a burglar. He had the keys; I had heard him use them. Why did he only pass through the flat and not live there? Perhaps he worked long hours – people do, who have work – and could only find time to move his belongings at night. My wife told me I was complicating things with my questions. All in time would be revealed, for places to live are too valuable, too desperately sought after, to remain empty or only partially inhabited for long.

I searched all night for sleep. At first light, it found me.

I had intended – for it was a fine day – to go for a walk on Burbage Moor, but I felt, upon waking, a weakness in my limbs, a dilution of my strength, and the prospect of the journey by bus, the long wait while cars rushed past, exhausted and depressed me. I made instead a couple of slow circuits of Ruskin Park, walking my shadow as other old men walk their dogs. I tried not to look at the scorched trees on Parkwood Springs, at the dry-ski slope covered in junk and rubble. The park, at least, is still maintained by local people and the children's play area has not been completely vandalised. Then again, the familiar slogan spray-painted into the pavements left me disinclined to look down as I walked. I sent my gaze for refuge into the trees. Their upper boughs swung free and undefiled.

That evening I dined at a fellow countryman's home in Crosspool. It is a grander place than mine, for my friend had resumed his practice as a family doctor upon coming to Sheffield. I wanted to reminisce about old times; he would talk only of the news, the flotillas around the coast, both official and unofficial, at their crusade of deterrence.

My friend drove me back to Walkley. I had told him nothing about the noises in the house or the mysterious comings and goings. It had been a relief to forget them for a while.

I stood in my kitchen, listening, and heard no sounds from above. Once again (oh, the rising and falling, the back-and-forth, of a long life) I prepared myself for bed and lay with my eyes closed, trying to keep my mind as windswept and blank as a beach dragged clean by the sea.

A drop of water broke on my cheek. I cried out and sat up in bed. I turned on the light. I could see no wetness on the ceiling. Had it even come from there? Instinctively I had wiped off the water with my sleeve; perhaps I had imagined it.

I lay back down, but my heart would not settle and I stared at the pale, empty plain above me. At last, wearily, I turned out the light, and almost the instant my head returned to the pillow, a second drop splashed my right eyelid.

Getting up, half raging, I turned on all the lights and stood on my bed to touch the ceiling. Was it damp? It was hard to be sure. Perhaps all I felt was the cool of the emulsion. Had the new occupant left a tap running? I should have taken a contact number off him in case of just such an emergency. Was it an emergency? A couple of drops of water (there was no sign of any elsewhere in the flat), what did that amount to or portend? Having no alternative, but unable to bear the insult, the anticipated shock, of more water on my face, I was obliged for the first time to lie on my wife's side of the bed, having placed a plastic bowl on the mattress where my pillow ought to be.

A drop fell into the bowl. Then another.

I hauled myself up the stairs, knocked loudly on the door of the flat. I got down on my knees to look through the keyhole and my eye swam in darkness. I pressed my ear against the door in case I might hear running water, or the overflowing of a bath, but I heard nothing.

Back in my flat, the water drops came more frequently

now, welling out of a stain in the ceiling above my bed. It was impossible to call my landlord at two in the morning, so I lay beside the tutting bowl watching the stain on the ceiling expand. My last thought, as the sleep of exhaustion washed over me, was that it looked like a human shadow.

★

I awoke four hours later in an instant state of alarm. However, the stain on the ceiling appeared not to have grown. There was only a thin film of water in the plastic bowl. I rinsed it away in the bathroom sink and replaced the bowl on my mattress in case the leak should resume. It was still early, but I had turned on my telephone to call my landlord when I heard motion in the stairwell. I flung on my dressing-gown and opened my door to find the landlord already there.

We gaped at each other.

'I was about to knock,' he said.

'Do you know what is happening? There is water coming through my ceiling.'

This appeared not to surprise him. 'Is it still coming?' he asked. 'The boards up there are soaked through.'

'It rained on my face.'

'Must be a pipe. I've a plumber coming.'

'Is the man who is renting the flat up there?'

'*Him.*' My landlord's face darkened. 'You won't see him again. Lucky I don't report him, only it'd reflect badly on me… I told him, soon as I knew what he were up to, I said I'm not having that in one of my rentals. Ten to a room they'll have 'em. Pretend it's just for him and the missus, and before you know it there's loads of 'em, four to a floor, mattress to mattress. At this rate we'll be overrun. Of course I'm not looking at you, but this new lot, I mean we're full, there's no way, I said to him, no way I'll have illegals under my roof.'

I observed the quaking of his jowls, the indignation of a good man put upon by iniquity. There were beads of sweat on his upper lip and on the flanks of his nostrils, and when he had finished speaking, he wiped the edges of his mouth with his thumb knuckle.

'How did you find out,' I asked, 'what he was planning?'

Before my landlord spoke, every atom in my body knew the answer.

'Well they drowned, dint they? Poor buggers. English Channel. Tried to get across in a bloody dinghy… I had my doubts, you see. I waited for him to turn up, just an hour ago, outside. I knew he were coming at nights. I got out the car, I said "What's going on, why've you not moved in, and what with all them beds?" Cause I have my keys, you see, I have to keep a set. He wept. I'm not kidding. He wept and said they'd all drowned. Been washed up on a beach, whole family.'

I watched my landlord. He is not a bad man. His eyes looked over and above and around me.

'So,' I said, 'there is nobody living in the flat?'

He looked straight at me then, sharply. 'Well obviously not.'

He made a few more utterances, about the damp, about the floorboards, all the while wiping his hands on the pockets of his trousers. I was no longer listening, and it was a relief when he left me alone with the silence upstairs.

I ascended slowly, leaning on the stair-rail, and placed my open palm on the front-door. I knew, with absolute clarity and horror, that the presence, corporeal or otherwise, that I had imagined in that flat was no such thing. It was absence. It was the negation of everything that had brought that family to Europe, of the hope that had driven them to the sea. Hope is the ghost that we dare not lay to rest.

I told you at the beginning that this is a very unsatisfactory story. The plumber, when he came, found no source for the water. Wherever the leak had come from, it had stopped. I lacked the courage to ask him whether the water had been fresh or salt.

In its traditional form, there is something comforting about the ghost story. It suggests, after all, that death is not the end, that something of the personality survives. How abjectly I have wished that this were true. When my wife's presence faded, like a fragrance, from the rooms where she had lived and where she had done her dying, I longed to see her ghost – for a sudden and untraceable scent of flowers – for a white feather in the centre of my pillow; any portent that might rescue her from oblivion. But the great wave took her. She lies fathoms deep in forgetting. I talked to her then, and talk to her still, but do not for one moment think that she is by my side. I do not know if I can bear this, but I know that I must try. For the greatest challenge – that we must answer by living – is accepting to love what dies.

The Time Is Now

Naomi Frisby

9 January 2019

RACHEL'S HEART THUMPS AS she runs across the street. She grips her coat, clasping it together, hoping it muffles the sound. With her head down, she steps onto the tram at the last set of doors. Her arm jars as her suitcase bumps against something. She tugs at it without looking back.

'Fucking hell,' a woman shouts.

The suitcase moves smoothly again. Rachel continues walking.

'She could've broken my foot,' the woman shouts down the carriage.

Rachel sits on one of the pull-down seats facing sideways and stares out of the window. Her heartbeat reverberates through her body.

The tram sets off. Rachel gazes at the view she's seen thousands of times before. The terraced houses. The trees that hide the brown-bricked council estates tucked away from the main road. The high rises on either side of the track as it runs up the middle of the dual carriageway, climbing one of Sheffield's seven hills.

She's tired although she slept the sleep of the dead last night. Her new heart felt light, almost hollow; its rhythmic clunking unexpectedly soothing.

At the university stop, a crowd gets on and people jostle for seats. Rachel pulls her suitcase in front of her so a woman can manoeuvre a pushchair into the space. The toddler looks at Rachel and Rachel smiles. The child starts to cry. Rachel turns to face the window again.

She doesn't know what's happened to her old heart. She hasn't heard from Christie or Adam or Louisa. They already feel like her past; people she used to be close to who've grown apart and moved on.

As the tram travels the length of West Street it starts to rain. The passengers in Rachel's carriage begin to fidget. Brollies appear and coats are zipped. The windows steam up.

They pass Ponds Forge and she feels in her coat pocket for her phone. She promised her dad she'll call him when she gets to London. There are no notifications on her lock screen.

Rachel pulls up her hood and gets off the tram at the stop for the station. The amphitheatre's directly in front of her. She stands and waits, hoping to see herself walking up the steps with Christie, but nothing happens. She turns to cross the tracks to the back entrance of the station. Her final view of the city centre is framed by steel-grey clouds.

Once she's placed her suitcase on the baggage rack and found her seat on the 10.29 to St. Pancras, Rachel empties her pockets – phone, lip gloss, purse, headphones – and shoves her coat onto the rack above her head. As the train pulls out of the station, the window obscured by the rain, Rachel opens the band's WhatsApp and types one word: Sorry.

8 January 2019

Rachel throws the box into the room.

'Who wants it?' she says, then leans against the door frame, arms folded.

The rest of the band are as far from each other as it's possible to be. Louisa's behind the drums. Adam cradles his guitar, sitting tight against the wall as though he's trying to merge into it. Christie picks at the purple varnish on her fingernails, her feet resting on her bass guitar case.

Rachel hasn't seen any of them since last week. She's ignored their texts and phone calls, refused to answer the front door, told her housemates and her boss she was ill and needed to rest.

'You come for attention?' says Christie. She doesn't look up.

Rachel stares at Christie. At her tight curls, at her light brown skin, at her long fingers. Rachel feels nothing.

'Is someone going to tell me what the fuck's going on?'

Louisa comes out from behind the kit and stands by the box. 'What's in it?' she says.

When Rachel doesn't answer, Louisa bends down and flips the clasps.

'Jesus Christ,' she shouts.

She kicks the box. It screeches along the floor, hits Adam's feet and judders to a stop. Louisa pushes past Rachel.

'Animal,' says Louisa before she lets the door swing back. Rachel doesn't flinch.

Adam leans his guitar against the wall, lifts the heart from the box and cradles it. He glances at Rachel, his hair obscuring one eye.

'I can't believe you're doing this,' he says.

Still Rachel doesn't respond.

The heart pulses in Adam's hands. He strokes it, shushes it. When his tears fall onto it, it shivers.

Rachel's growing bored but she waits.

Christie jumps up, strides across the room and stands over Adam. She looks at Rachel.

'Is this what you want?' she says.

She lunges for the heart. Adam closes his grip so Christie only manages to clasp a chunk of it. The heart pounds, its beat echoing through Christie and Adam's arms. Rachel watches, curious as to who will take it.

'Shit,' shouts Christie. She shakes her hand, sucks her index finger.

Adam examines his palm as blood drips from it. The heart writhes and snaps on the floor.

'Love bites,' says Rachel and leaves.

3 January 2019

Rachel opens her chest and removes her heart. It's pounding so hard she has to form a cage with her hands to prevent it from jumping. She places it in the wooden box then picks up her new heart and fits it behind her ribcage.

She shudders. Goosebumps rise on her arms and her legs. She breathes out frost. It feels as though winter has settled inside her body. She closes her chest, pulls the duvet up to her neck and waits.

The heart clangs. It sounds like the pipes in an old house as the hot water begins to flow. Rachel doesn't feel any warmer. There's a numbness to her body, although when she wiggles her fingers and toes they respond straight away. She makes the shape of a snow angel to check her arms and legs, then twists her head from side to side. Walking around her bedroom makes the heart clank louder. She puts a t-shirt on and does another circuit. Loud. A jumper. Still loud. A jacket. Slightly quieter. She switches the jacket for her winter coat with the fleece lining. Still audible but could probably be explained away by the double zip-pulls clashing or her keys jangling in her pocket. Rachel takes off the coat and gets back into bed.

For the last two weeks, she's opened the box every day, left prints on the steel as she's run her fingers along it.

Magazines, billboards and the TV have promised new year, new you, but Rachel holds the power to make it happen.

Band practice is a disaster. They start with a long-term favourite, their cover of 'Separated by Motorways' by The Long Blondes.

'You're flat,' says Adam, as the rhythm section trails off underneath his words.

'I'm not. I'm perfectly in tune.'

'Not your pitch,' says Adam. 'Your delivery. You could be singing the phone book.'

They start the song again, making it to the end, but Adam shakes his head at her. They try another one. Adam stops them before they get to the second verse.

'I'm making an effort. I am,' says Rachel. She feels like a petulant teenager.

'Perhaps we should call it a night,' says Adam.

'I'm leaving anyway,' says Rachel.

'Are you okay?' Christie touches Rachel's arm.

'There's no need to go,' says Adam. 'You're just having a bad day. First rehearsal back. Let's get a pint.'

'No, I'm leaving,' says Rachel. 'Sheffield. I'm leaving Sheffield.'

'What? When?' says Christie.

'Next week.'

Louisa moves out from behind the drums and joins Christie and Adam as they surround Rachel.

'Were you planning on mentioning this at any point?' says Christie.

'I'm mentioning it now.'

Rachel is completely calm. The heart clashes but it doesn't race. There's no pounding in her ears, no dizziness. It's done.

At home, she opens the lid of the wooden box to exchange the hearts again; she won't need the steel one until the day she leaves.

As she picks up her flesh and blood heart, she notices there are marks on it, bruises. She touches her finger to a small, dark dot. A memory of the first time her and Louisa fell out. Year 10. They didn't speak for two weeks. Rachel was jealous of Louisa's new friendship with a boy who'd transferred to their school. At the time it was devastating but now it feels distant, remote.

A bigger patch triggers a vision of the end of her last long-term relationship. Her boyfriend sitting on the kitchen floor, his head dipped. She sees it as though she's watching TV; a drama belonging to someone else.

She turns the heart over. There's a deep stain with cracks running through it. She places her palm against it and there's her mum in the back garden at home. She's sitting on a blanket, blowing bubbles through a wand. It's sunny. Rachel sees the bubbles her toddler self is trying to catch, but they either dissolve or she misses them. She's giggling.

Rachel moves her palm from her heart to her cheek. Her face is dry. She puts the heart down and touches both of her cheeks. No tears. The ache that usually comes with recollections of her mum is absent too. And then she knows that she can't switch the hearts back again. New year, new you.

Christmas Day 2018

The cooking's well underway when Rachel arrives at her dad's house. Even though it's only the two of them, he still does a roast with all the trimmings. Rachel puts the Yule Log she's made into the fridge and wishes her dad a Merry Christmas. He hugs her.

'He's been,' he says and nods towards the living room.

'Has he?' Rachel smiles. 'He stopped by my house too.'

She holds up a bag.

Her dad gets them both a beer while Rachel arranges the presents into a pile in front of the tree. She's bought him the slippers he asked for, a copy of *Fresh India*, a packet of brandy snaps and 'The Story So Far: The Best of Def Leppard' on vinyl. She's tried to get her dad into streaming, but he says it just doesn't feel right.

They alternate opening gifts until there's only one left.

'Go on,' says her dad.

Rachel pulls one end of the red ribbon tied in a bow on the top. It slips apart and she pushes it off the paper. She peels the Sellotape from each end, unfolds the wrapping, then loosens the last piece on the long edge. Inside there is a heavy wooden box. She runs her fingers across the initials carved into the top. Her initials. She hesitates. Her breath is shallow and she feels sick.

Her dad watches as she lifts the lid. Rachel gasps. It's exactly what she wanted. She removes the steel heart from the box. It's the size of her fist and much lighter than she imagined. There are arteries protruding from the top and both sides but otherwise it's smooth, perfectly cast, polished and cold. She shakes the heart; it's silent. She taps it with her fingers and then raps her knuckles against it. The sound it makes is flat, dull, lifeless. On the back, at the bottom, there's a trademark: Made in Sheffield. She turns to her dad.

'It's perfect,' she says.

7 October 2018

The band get together at Christie's for the first episode of the new *Doctor Who*. Some of the filming took place at Park Hill and they're hoping to catch a glimpse of the outside of the flat. They heat up oven pizzas then arrange themselves in the living room. Rachel and Christie sit on the sofa. Louisa joins them but moves to the floor instead, using the sofa as a backrest. Adam lies across the carpet in front of the TV. The end of *Countryfile* plays on the screen.

'Best Doctor?' says Christie.

'Tennant, obvs,' says Rachel.

'Reserving judgement till the end of the episode,' says Louisa.

Adam rolls over to face them. 'You can't judge on one episode,' he says.

'Watch me.'

'You can't,' he says.

'Who's yours?' says Christie. She waves a piece of pizza in Adam's direction.

'Tom Baker. Classic.'

'Before your time,' says Christie. 'Before all of our times.'

'There's these magic inventions called videos and DVDs and the internet. They allow you to watch things created before you were born.'

'Is he mansplaining?' says Christie. 'Is he?' She looks at Rachel.

'It's starting,' says Rachel. She grabs the remote and turns the volume up.'

They're all quiet as they watch the opening few minutes. PC Yazmin Khan arrives to see what Ryan's found in the woods.

'So many people of colour,' says Christie.

'Yorkshire accents,' says Rachel.

The Doctor crashes into the train and searches for her sonic screwdriver.

'Pockets!' shout Rachel, Christie and Louisa.

'This is so good,' says Rachel.

Adam's quiet, elbow bent, head resting on his hand, watching. In the show, a white van drives past Bramall Lane and turns onto a cobbled side street.

'Where's that?' says Louisa.

'Not in that part of Sheffield,' says Christie.

Adam looks back at them. 'Can we just watch it?' he says.

They do. They stay quiet. Even when the bus station across from where they're sitting right now appears on screen. Even when Jodie Whittaker says 'would of' instead of 'would have'. They stay quiet right up until there's a drunk man in a backstreet throwing salad from his kebab at an alien.

'That's the most Sheffield thing I've ever seen,' says Christie.

Rachel disagrees but she doesn't say so. The most Sheffield thing in this episode is The Doctor casting, forging, welding her own sonic screwdriver from Sheffield steel. It's all Rachel thinks about as the rest of the episode takes place. When The Doctor delivers the line 'Swiss Army Sonic, now with added Sheffield steel,' Rachel cheers as tears flow down her face.

August 2018

Rachel stops in the middle of the pavement.

'Fucking hell, love,' says a man as he pushes past her.

Her heart races and her breaths are rasping. People dart around her as she staggers across the footpath and leans against the nearest building. There's something wrong with her eyes or her brain or maybe both. She places her palm against the wall and breathes deeply. She forces herself to look up, to scan the street. The thing that walked past her has disappeared, but Rachel knows with absolute certainty that what she saw was real. In the five years since her mum died, Rachel's seen her on several occasions – walking down the street, in cafes, in clothes shops. Today though, Rachel didn't see her mum, she saw herself.

It starts to happen more often. On the tram, at work, in the pub, climbing the hill to Christie's flat. She's there, like a bad cover version, wearing clothes Rachel would no longer wear and hair styles she's long since discarded. Sometimes old Rachel is in front of current Rachel. On other occasions they pass each other, locking eyes for a few seconds. After each meeting, Rachel wishes she'd said something. Asked why she's here, what she wants.

Rachel doesn't tell anyone, not even Christie. She searches the internet for descriptions of similar visions, but all the results are for people who've seen themselves in dreams. These aren't dreams, they're nightmares.

She starts taking a different route to work, to home, to Christie's flat. It's successful for a while but then she's back, only now she's the Rachel of a few weeks earlier.

One Saturday she asks Christie if she ever thinks about leaving.

'Here?'

'Yes,' says Rachel.

'No,' says Christie. 'Why would I uproot my entire life? For what?'

And then Rachel can see it all spooling out in front of her. Babies. A mortgage. Older versions of herself walking the same streets over and over and over again.

27 September 2017

The date was Rachel's suggestion, but the location was Christie's and now Rachel's regretting saying yes to it. They could've gone to the cinema or for a meal. Instead, they're climbing the steps by the amphitheatre so they can walk up to Norfolk Park. Halfway up Rachel can feel sweat pooling in her lower back. She stops and turns so it looks as though she's admiring the view.

'It's better from the park,' shouts Christie.

She's almost at the top. Rachel raises her hand in acknowledgement.

'Are you okay?' says Christie.

'Yeah, just –'

'You forget how steep it is when you do it all the time.'

Christie waits while Rachel catches up and they climb the rest of the steps together. As they walk along Norfolk Road, they talk briefly about their day but soon they're on to music.

Rachel grew up listening to pop, her bedroom covered with posters of Britney and Five and Geri Halliwell and Robbie Williams. When Louisa moved from a different class into Rachel's science group in Year 9, they christened their new friendship by listening to indie bands. A headphone each, hidden by their hair, iPod stashed in Louisa's trouser pocket. In a good lesson they could get through an entire album. When they formed a band in Year 11 there was no discussion about the type of music they were going to play and in the years since there's been little change. But now Rachel loves Christie's taste; it's so much broader than her own and is one of the reasons she wanted her in the band. Christie introduced Rachel to Missy Elliot and Massive Attack and John Coltrane and reminded her that pop music exists and that she loves it.

As they reach the park, they discuss the directions the band could take, Rachel's voice getting louder and louder as she bounds along next to Christie.

'I've never been here before,' says Rachel.

They walk along Turkey Oak Avenue. Rachel looks up at the trees, their branches long and twisted.

'Never?' says Christie. 'How long have you lived here?'

'My entire life. On the other side of the city.'

They follow the path to the top of the park, discussing whether or not they think Louisa and Adam will agree to try new things. The trees disappear from one side of the path and the park opens out, sloping down in front of Rachel and Christie.

'Wow,' says Rachel.

'Wait until we get further round,' says Christie.

They carry on past the visitor centre towards the archway. 'Here,' says Christie.

As Rachel stands and looks, Christie takes two bottles of beer from her bag, flips the tops off and hands one to Rachel.

'It's alright, isn't it?' says Christie.

She takes a swig of her beer.

'Amazing,' says Rachel.

Christie sits on the grass and Rachel joins her. They drink their beers in silence, looking across at the outline of the city. The horizon begins to glow yellow. Rachel's heartbeat echoes in her ears. Her hand rests on the grass, millimetres from Christie's. The sky deepens to orange and then red. Without looking away from the sunset, Rachel stretches her little finger until it touches Christie's. They lock hands.

'I love this city when the sun goes down,' says Christie.

She turns to Rachel and kisses her for the first time.

Scrap

Karl Riordan

A LOUD KNOCKING WAKES me; the silver badge on his helmet is bright as a torch in the frosted glass arch of the front door. *Lie still, hold your breath*, I tell myself. Thank fuck the curtains are permanently closed. I slide off the sofa trying to avoid the junk metal and stripped wire strewn across the floor. His walkie-talkie screeches, followed by some garbled talking. On hands and knees, I crawl to the stairs before he thinks of flipping the letter box and peering in. Maybe he has already and is playing some kind of mind game.

I take the stairs three at a time, avoiding the ninth and the floorboard on the landing. Colin opens his attic room door as I'm about to tap. He places a calloused palm across my mouth and whispers: 'They'll go away. It's a waiting game.'

I nod and he takes back his hand. We go to the front bedroom window to investigate. Colin creeps to the window and looks up into the car wing mirror we'd fixed to the wall, angled to show who was at the door. We thought of this after the TV licensing incident. The larger bottom telly was acting as a stand for the middle one that worked occasionally. Top tier was the reliable black-and-white portable. She turned up dressed in a Royal Mail jacket and nabbed us. Afternoon TV is good for no one.

There's no longer a copper at the door but through the net curtain I can make out his sidekick at the wheel in the car parked across the road, scribbling into a notebook. That indicates they'll be back.

Now, where's the knocker-upper? Probably round the back taking a look at the sink full of pots, which were mostly Colin's. They're like that, the police, always judging. It's always telling that they live outside the community they serve.

At first I tried to keep on top of the mucky dishes, have some self-respect, but didn't see the point after about three weeks. I once counted thirteen cups he'd collected around his chair, not to mention the take-away cartons.

What will this copper make of the sacks? These were full of non-ferrous metal we'd collected over the months to have a big weigh-in. The house had evolved into a kind of factory system. We'd dismantle in the living room over beer and scotch and, when bagged, the metals would be moved to the kitchen. Aye, I'll bet he's writing 'suspicious sacks' into his notepad right now.

'We ought to shift those sacks, Col.'

'Today, we'll load up what we've got.'

'Let's make sure we do.'

'Look, the other cop's come back.'

His pal winds down the window and old Peeping-Tom chats to him, hands him something. He stands straight, turns around and looks up at our window while talking into his radio.

'Get back, Col, he'll clock us.'

'Calm thi sen, they've nowt on us. They'll be away in a min.'

'We should clear that kitchen. It must look like we've been robbing the fucking diocese.'

'But we haven't.'

'Aye, but you know what t' cops are like.'

'We've to be as sly as they are.'

I look and they're both in the car now.

'What're they waiting for?'

'Kenny, shut the fuck up.'

Colin sits on the edge of my bed and starts to roll a cigarette. If that's not bad enough he starts to warm up a block of hash.

'Fuck's sake, man, not now and not in my room!'

He wraps it back into the cling-film and sparks up just the tobacco. I go back to the window and they've driven away. I snatch the roll-up from Colin's lips and take a drag.

I was in on the scrap for Colin's mate, Sneaky Keith, who had been convicted of driving offences and was serving a spell in Doncatraz. I wondered how he was coping as he was on a bottle of 'gold-watch' every night and I always noticed the DT's kick in at about half-six.

We both met Keith at a previous rental after he'd been kicked out of his marital home. He got the bottom room; what it must be like to be forty and have to go back into a bedsit.

Keith wanted to make enough from collecting scrap then start up a knife-grinding business from the back of the van. He needed a driver and Colin just went along with the scheme. By the second week he'd persuaded us both to fiddle the electric and gas meters. I just nodded – if caught, I'd play dumb. Week three and the York stone from the cellar and back garden path had disappeared.

Sneaky Keith, aka Cockney Keith, claimed to have been a top-class waiter in various London restaurants. He went on about his celebrity encounters; he claimed Shirley Bassey had flirted with him, and that her language was as filthy as a brickie's.

Then there was the night we'd nipped out to pick up a pizza. We got back and he'd gone out, so we both ate an extra slice of his. Then came this loud kicking at the door and in rolls Keith just out of Casualty with his fingers taped up in splints looking like a fucking scarecrow.

He told us he owed 200 quid to Pop Stoker who'd chased him up the stairs with a baseball bat. Pop had swung like Babe Ruth and took a chunk from one of the spindles on the handrail. Keith managed to protect his head with his hands, and we had to spend the next few weeks feeding him like a bairn.

Just after Keith got locked up we decided to do a moonlight flit and here we are at number 4, Palmer Street. Even now when we're out on the scrap we're wary of bumping into Duncan, the ex-landlord. He'd been a footballer who'd used his fame to build up a haulage firm where he made his money. In retirement he'd gone into the rental business converting large properties into magnolia boxes, extracting as much profit as possible. We'd often spot his Range Rover, private reg: D20 UNC, on his inspection of rentals either showing people around or serving notice of eviction.

Our grey van is parked at the top of the road and uninsured. I wait for Colin to pull up around the back so we could load up our small fortune. He has this knack of being able to roll a fag with one hand and still drive. His wheezing is getting worse. We select our scrap dealer by trawling the estates, looking out for white goods dumped in gardens.

There's a skip with 'greedy boards' so we pull up and fish through the junk. It seems to be a renovation job by the sound of hammering inside the house. All we get are some old metal window frames and a buckled racing bike but it all adds up.

'Let's get this weighed in, then I've a little job planned,' Colin says.

'What now?'

'Remember that garage off Doncaster Road?'

'Aye.'

'Well he'll pay twenty quid to take away plastic bumpers.'

'We can't weigh them in.'

'I know a spot near a railway banking we can tip.'

'That's illegal.'

'One-off.'

'Your trouble is you've no conscience.'

The man at the garage is a wiry-looking fellow with a stoop and scaly eyes. He takes us through the workshop where a young apprentice watches us with suspicion, chewing on his sandwich. The stench of oil hits the back of my throat. There's a small mountain of car bumpers in the back yard.

'Can you do this regular?'

'Maybe once a month,' Colin says.

'We'll pay fifteen per removal.'

'You said twenty – I've got petrol to cover and a man to pay.'

'Tha'll break me, but keep this to thi sen. Cheers, cock.'

It takes us an hour to get to the disused railway banking and we have to act fast fighting these bumpers, flinging them as far as possible. It's over quickly and I'll try to talk him out of it over the next month. He'd picked up tips from Sneaky Keith. I was sick of hearing 'Keith said this,' or 'Keith said that'. I want the old Colin back but keep this to myself. This was short-term as Keith would be back out in a couple of months and I reckoned I'd be brushed aside.

We push on into the afternoon after a pub lunch on the 114 quid we'd made on the non-ferrous. Colin orders a lager shandy and we eat a two-for-one meal deal of gammon and egg. We use the pub toilets to scrub away the black stuff from the bumper job.

'That landlord's a grumpy bastard. See him clocking us?'

'Quick enough to take the money.'

We select a new scrap dealer who we've never used for the next job Colin has planned. The van is mainly full of white goods and I detect a scheme unfolding. He parks at the edge of a demolished estate which is deserted. All I can see are bricks.

'There's nowt here of value, Col.'

'Take a closer look.'

'Aye, bricks and rubble.'

'And what's that tell thee?'

'That you're taking the piss.'

'Follow me.'

He backs up to a mound of bricks and debris. I watch as he opens the back of the van, then the oven doors on some of the cookers and the fridge we'd picked up from an old wifey that wouldn't let us away. Colin starts to fill up the mod-cons with bricks and rubble and then I twig. The wily old bastard! Seems obvious when you think about it. I laugh at the plan and don't feel half as bad about the bumper job. I mean, these dealers will try it on and it's just getting a bit of your own back. We're the ones putting in the graft while they sit on their sprawling arses counting the readies. The one that morning was such a prick, with his chunky gold bracelet and thick knotted tie. His plooky face made me want to retch, especially the one on his cheek that probably had a fucking heartbeat. We drove away casual and slow at first, my arse twitching until we got around the corner.

'We've only got away with it,' I tell Colin.

'I thought we'd fucked it then. See his face when counting out the notes?'

'Aye, that and disappearing into the back office for an age.'

'I reckon they'd have let that rabid Alsatian off its rope, feeding on thi shin for dinner.'

We decide to take the rest of the day off after making

another 78 quid. I feel around in the side of the door pocket, slip a random cassette into the player which must have been left by the previous owner. Johnny Cash sings 'One Piece at a Time'. I think old Johnny's got the right idea and we both sing along.

'Let's just have a quick look around here,' Colin says.

We drive into a large DIY warehouse car park; over at the far corner is a skip full of old metal shelving. You dancer! There's easy a vanload. We manage to stack up with an air of casualness and we get no bother off anybody. I figured we were doing them a good turn by removing the buckled shelving. Where I grew up any skip would be an opportunity for the neighbourhood to have a clear out. We pack it all in with little room for anything else. The struts take the length of the van and we have to manoeuvre the longer pieces to rest between our heads.

I push in another home recorded cassette that plays Townes Van Zandt. I guess the name of the song is 'Nothing' from the regular refrain. Colin starts to whistle and I see this lucky find has him ready for the weekend.

We pull out onto the main street of an ex-mining village and I roll two fags lighting both at the same time and hand one over.

'Gis thi lighter, I've gone out.'

I hand it over and Colin clicks the Zippo on his thigh.

It could have been minutes, maybe longer. There's a small crowd looking over from the shops. Colin had ran into the back of a parked vehicle. My legs are now shoved to my right like a coy woman getting out of a taxi and the left wing of the van is lifted – magnified. The car we'd hit had an old man in it who didn't appear to be moving.

The shelving had shot forward and Colin is bleeding from the head. The metal was caging us in. He's still moving and lifts his head. There's blood on his teeth when he smiles at me.

'I think we're fucked here. Can you get out?'

It takes a shove, but I manage to force open the door.

'Aye.'

'Go, there's no point us both copping it.'

'You alright?'

'I'll have a headache.'

'Sure?'

'Go!'

There are faces pressed against the barber shop window and I realise a tethered dog has been yapping for a while outside the Post Office. Townes has now moved onto 'Fare Thee Well Miss Carousel'. I could easily slip away before the emergency services show but something tells me to stay.

'Kenny, shift man!'

He repeats himself but I climb back up into the van and reassemble the metal shelving. I sit back in the leather passenger seat that sighs and try to light up a tab end. I feel around in my jacket pockets for my lighter then flick the duff butt into the street. I reach over and rewind the tape. It squeaks as it whirrs backwards. I hear the sirens first and press play before the flashing blues come into view.

The first ambulance man attending the scene wants to get us out of our van and into theirs. They put Colin on a stretcher and raise him with the hydraulic foot pump. I insist on walking, keeping close to his side. They keep asking for his name and mine and did he know who the Prime Minister was?

'I'm Colin, 26 years old and my mate's a hitcher. Thatcher.'

Long Fainting/Try Saving Again

Tim Etchells

A true story of Endland (sic)

I

MARTHA'S DAUGHTER (GINA) WAS 12 yrs age when she probably by accident but possibly on purpose uploaded herself to internet and disappeared from her bedroom b4 tea time. Martha tried yelling up stairs and all that, saying food was on the table fucks sake get down here now before it goes cold but Gina dint show up again anytime soon so the rest of the kids just got straight to tucking in and ate her share as well as their own, here we go here we go.

*

Days past and turned to weeks and then they (the weeks) turned to months and G's brothers were not slow to claimed her bedroom and her sisters claimed her best trainers and for reasons no one really understood the neighbours' basic bitch nieces took the nicest of her clothes.

  G's dad was that kind of bloke that was long gone since long time and cunt care bout anything cept living what he called La Vida Fucking Loca, but when he herd news about Gina he came straight back to the town of S____. He came rocking down from the Mountains (?) with what looked like a suntan and a new wife or possibly gf, 'to see what he could help with find his daughter'. Only when the answer was resoundingly like 'nothing' did he go back up there (to place he lived again), with his head lowered down, his poor heart broke in the pieces and nothing but his grief full intact.

Meanwhile Martha was like Absolut Wretched, worried sick for her poor digitised girl, climbing walls barefoot w/out safety gear, watching the backdoor and also the front for her daughter's return, weeping and listening, checking their broadband bill for sines of activity or life, the waking hours a non-stop listless listing of questions w/out answers, wretched reasons and non-reasons, all to no avail.

★

Time passed. In the town (of S____) Martha watched her screen each day for sines of Gina, while outside the sunshine lost its fight with the sundry forces of shadows, bureaucratic incompetence, boredom, pollution and proliferate dog shit.

It was a hard time for her and fam in general. When the millennium came her Mum passed away while one of her sisters died of nostalgia, another of greed, another of rent arrears, another of syphilis, another of blackmail, another of malnutrition. Her brother had a accident at work and was confined to a wheelbarrow.

Martha built a shrine to her missing daughter, ink-jetted photos and a printout of her browser history pinned all over the living room wall, a scented candle burning and a lock of Gina's hair pressed between pages of an old SUDUKO magazine whereof M thought (wrongly) that the numbers in the puzzles might be some kind of lucky.

Around the same time there was one of those slow and mysterious declensions to the tags marking the bus shelters and underpass walls in the city that happened in Endland (sic) in those dayze, whereby VILE / OK MELT / HEDZ / JERK

/ VOTE and SKEEMER were slowly edged out by the new names that no one really recognised at first like LO / WIDE / SMURFIT / SLIMEZ and later FWIW / JCRW / TWAKTIKS and O. The last of these, perhaps simplest of tags as cld be ever imagined, was soon appearing all round the whole town, more or less each and every wall in that place apparently infected with its wide void and profligate gape – O O O O O O – like a scream maybe that had disperse into the bitter architectures of S____, or some kind of desperate abstracted and communal gasping for air.

★

Martha found a job in one of the groups clearing rubble from WWII bomb sites that still for some reason seemed to riddle the town centre. It was hard labour, paid in old money and the work had to be conducted entirely in black and white, requiring that she and other workers each day spent time and effort before the shift started to put on appropriate make-up and retro clothes (also black and white). Martha liked the job tho and also liked what she called 'the camaraderie's of people' etc and how they were supposedly working together to build a new world debased on commonly held principles and a desire to end the hardships, divisions and struggles of the recent past.

On the chain gang Martha met a woman called Louise, another idealist whose eyes were flashing diamonds, whose scent was cinnamon, a decent deodorant and pride, whose voice was an old river song that dredged up the kind of feelings and complicated emotions that had long ago been left there under the water and/or had accumulated in the layers of thick silt and mud. The two of them fell in love, set up house together in a house they sub-letted on a nearby estate. It was sinful what they did, at least as far as their neighbours were concerned, but that lot were fucking idiots mostly that got their news for real off of Facebook and had other stuff to deal with/problems of their own.

Outside the city boundary meanwhile things were volatile and the actual front line of what they sometimes called the current conflict kept moving around so you could never really know for sure where it was safe to go out and where it wasn't. Mortars – probly fired by western special forces – rained down constantly on what they said was insurgent holdouts (ie places people were still living) in Hillsborough and The Manor, sending thick towers of horrible smoke rising right up into the air that could be seen for miles around and making it impossible for people to see where they were going.

The King of Endland (sic) himself tried to make a decree to stop the bombing but at the last minute they caught him and put him in a prison for ever.

Some pieces of the information are missing so please try to checking the connection. Some part of it have gone missing are missing. Try checking a connection.

★

Far off wheresoever he still claimed to live in the mountains, G's dad died of a suspected climbing accident that doctors would not confirm and then as the poets say 'his new wife/gf or whatever did a fucking runner', leaving Martha to pretty much pick up the pieces plus the tab for the funeral and other arrangements.

By the time it was all over and her ex was in the ground – morticians paid, service and speeches got thru, the unpacked pre-packed sandwiches either eaten or else slid from off of their plastic platters and down into the trash – M was technically bankrupt, a pauper in everything including her name, spinning empty plates, juggling bad debt from one card to another, only just making ends almost meet. One night when M was sleeping exhausted something snapped in her love (Louise) who then like packed her bags w/out warning and snuck out of town all alone on a Red Cross branded convoy that was equal parts refugees, battle-scarred war tourists and fighters in disguise.

Martha was heartbroken and subsequential months passed slowly. Smoke (from the bombs mentioned already) was any where and ever where in the town and therefore life was hard to see properly, the streets thick and tangled, the building submerged like C19th and industry.

In the fraught empty bed of her grieving (more her mum, two of her sisters, her vanished daughter and exiting lover than death of her largely useless ex-husband) M descended further each minute of each hour. Nite tremors. Heart sink as like a generalised direction of travel.

Daytime for her was a job whereby she had to lay a kind of horrible poisonous paste around town using her bare hands, working for the Pest Control people appointed by the council, spreading it (poisonous paste) on the kerbs and into the grime of piss-stained corners and up walls of alleyways and then (later) home cooking tasty/economical meals for her still surviving kids in the sadly depleted household of her life.

Night for M meanwhile was the colour black. The sound of rain and slurred uneasy voices. Cars driving too fast. Trash tangled in overgrown spaces that used to be gardens. Warm air from basement pumped thru the grease encrusted on ventilator grilles. Street washed in thick waves of Kremlin brand © aftershave. Moths in halogens of road-menders. Raves in warehouse under railway arches. Objects in nightmare arrangements. A violent scrabble of letters that could not anyhow be used to make words.

Sometimes dead of nite Martha thought she felt a kind of presence of her daughter – ghost Gina or spirit maybe – 'up there' somewhere / online or something, at least as she liked to describe it. Symptoms/delusions:

– a shiver sensation she had when a page loaded badly
– glitched advertisement
– faint tune or singing from invisible browser tab left open
– 404 Not Found

★

More part missing from the information in this part. Try to check in connections. The connection. Try checking the connection.

Once a clean river was in Endland. They had a trial the King of Endland. And after wards they chop off his head. Once there was a robot in Endland. They had a trial of a robots in Endland and after woods they sawed off its head.

II

When Gina came back – eventually and total unexpected from like no one knew how and no one know where – she was approximeatly (sic) 20 years old. Less time had passed on the Internet than it had for the rest of her fam or 'control group' (meaning the rest of the world) which is something that Einstein (the scientist not the singer/rapper) had once already long ago supposedly predicted in equations. In any case Gina looked different but still acted pretty much all the same incl same voice, much the same attitude, some of the same delinquent stare etc but other people had aged more. No one had a clue really what had happened to her during her long absent but the more people asked abt it the more she wunt discuss it no matter what/if you asked her questions not a Million times or more. The past was a locked room, she said,

92

a black hole or global warming, a topic not to be mentioned. It was a mystery but not that kind of mystery as other people found attractive or compelling, more like that kind as made them wary, distant, cold.

Old now ancient neighbours of the old neighbourhood waggled their tongues of cause to see her returned, and her sisters – now grown up and with husbands/bfs, kids and mental health problems of their own – acted jealous of her unspoken adventures and whatever, but nothing to be done.

Gina was strange. Life online had clearly left its toll on her attention span and vocabulary plus while she had information about almost anything, in another sense she seemed to know nothing at all. Martha said Gina was 'just like the kid she had been back then when she had 1st uploaded herself' but a yearning in the statement showed it wasn't really true. Gina tried to fit in the world as best she could when she came in it again, making bad jokes, making gang signs and drinking cold Old Beers like anyone else, but in true fact, if she ever heard the sound of distant modems there was soon a far off and far away look that came into her very haunted kind of eyes.

★

Despite all forces of alienation etc Martha nonetheless welcomed her daughter home and for a while G lived in peace and pieces there at her mums place, camping on the sofa and helping out with some jobs around the house.

In locality there were rumours of cause. Some said Gina was seen wandering naked at midnight and moonlight each night. Some that G was not really G, but instead a fraud/imposter come to reap illegal the family of its ill fortune. Some said that G was ghost or spirit, robot, android or ghoul. Or that G was only CGI. Some said that if you stared in G's eyes you could see the pixelated swirl of the internet she'd fallen so long years and years before. That in her heart was the song of a old school modem – hissing calling, crackling and bursting.

When G's mum Martha inevitably died of mostly unknown causes, it was G as then inherited all the little money and a pitiful amount that M had and her sisters stopped speaking to her in a jealous rage. And so it was according to what the poets say, that Gina exited the house, selling up and then moving henceforthly to a different place on a edge of the city (of S___) less filled up with other people's memories.

~~Missing information. Do not try searching. Do not try searching again.~~

~~Sometimes things are buried for a reason.~~

~~Once there was a Queen of Endland. There was a river underground in Endland. There was a river underground and car park underground in Endland. There was a Queen of Endland.~~

~~The wall of Karim Kebabs was covered in pictures of people that no one remembers, not even Shiv who manages the place for Karim. Kareem (alternatively spelled Karim, (Kahreem) or Kerim) (Arabic: كريم) is a common given name and surname of Arabic origin that means generous or noble. It should not be confused with Al-Karim (Arabic: الكريم), which is one of the 99 names of Allah, meaning The Most Generous. Karim is also a spelling of the similar, though much less common, name (Arabic: كرم), which is commonly spelled as Karam, Karem or Kerem. Another derivative name of (Arabic: أكرم) is Akram, meaning more generous~~

III

One night in a storm Gina took shelter in a pub that looked like it had once seen better dayze. The pub was run by a cruel Ogre (and also wife of the Ogre) in fact a hideous, man-like being that liked to eat ordinary human beings, especially infants and the children. It (the pub) was organised like a straightfwd converted mega franchise come Open-Plan Beer Zone & Video Jukebox Sky Sports and Karaoke Palace (also Microbrewery) that had long ago been abandoned by its supposedly natural olde clientele while the younger ladz and chicas of the area round it considered going there as an insult to their cosmopolitan dignity cos they and all their numerous mates etc sed proudly they 'only liked drinking in town'.

G was at first immediately captured by the Ogres and put to work in the pub. Night after night she had to worked her fingers into bones, wipe floor w hair, sluice out toilet from flood water and rats, manage out the worst of the smackheads and the morons, cooked bacon Snaks if needed for Ogre anytime in the fryer at 2000 degrees, kept a brite smile © on her face and generally listened to customers if they were talking to her etc keeping track of who was potentially a danger of attack, robbery, rape and worse. As each dawn approached G stood exhausted with skin stripped bare in the naked strip light of the pub bathroom, bar closed and strippers sent home, lamenting her fate and dead lookz and not much lolz left in her eyes.

She could neither read anymore, nor speak any normal language. She spoke the jargon of ogress and lived in perfect ignorance of all things in the world outside cos no TV but still she (Gina) dint stop having principles of virtue and of sweetness so natural as if was like she had been raised in the Court of the King of Endland or the most polite house of society. She had wore a skin dress made of tiger; her arms were half-naked what she worked all night to clean the floors.

Nontheless each night G was so unhappy wanted to escape and thought she would do any thing anything at all to escape the terrible ~~tavern~~ cavern.

~~Information missing. There is an problem with file and location it is saving to may have been changed or moved. Try saving again. Try saving again and again.~~

~~The text displayed may contain some errors. Let it go. Let fortune guide him. Her. Let's go back to S_____ to see what is happening~~

At closing time one night G was somehow elected (?) landlord of the pub by means or by the method of killing the Ogre and the wife of the Ogre (Ogress) when they were sleeping. Never was there more hideous figures than them (she thought) and she (Gina) killed them with fire they used to boil children in it and then that she killed them with stones the Ogre used to grind bones to make bread, then that she killed them with the Knife the Ogress used to cut the throats of domesticated animals and then that she killed them by trick trip and push them in the cellar, and then that she kill them push them in the deep well they cannot climb up out of it and then that she kill them with poison in their gruel that she was making them each morning from Aldi or Lidl and then.

~~There is a forest in Endland. Once there was a dire. Once there was a fire in Endland.~~
~~Place behind hills where each nite the many stars are fallen.~~

★

In her new job (ie as landlord of the pub) G got minimum wage and soon skipped away the worst of useless interior décor and other like gimmicks introduced by the Ogre and his wife Ogre (Ogress) as the previous managers. She it was that got rid of their blackboards for menu and jokes of the day, shelves of stupid books no one knows how to read, the cabinets of like fake 'mummified remains', paintball weapons, posters of Kardassians (sic), strippers etc, repainting the whole place, rebranding and re-opening again but w the old name (*The George and Dragon*) restored as replacement for the new smart ass self-conscious name that ogres had chosen and no one was ever able to remember.

There were certainly ups and downs to the pub business, hardships and dilemmas of all kind of cause incl supply and demand as well as staffing issues for all nite all day all nite shifts plus extra trouble managing reputation of the place (the pub) cos of all that happened there before (killing of Ogres, grinding of bones on the premises etc). But soon things was going alright with profits. Brewery happy and tax man contented and many a legendary and convivial evening of the estate was held in there including famed cabaret appearance of Led Dawson and Les Zeppelin, and the time regulars like Len and Rajni bet Marcella that Doreen wasn't wearing her hearing aid and all the many amount of hilarity that ensued.

★

Time passed in Endland (sic) with a few of what they call in that place 'good yrs' ©. Gina and her surviving sister(s) were reconciled. Her Mum's lover Louise came back round again, too late she did not know or hear that Martha had passed away. Anyway Louise was very very old by then and had that kindness and total fucking clarity that comes sometimes for people when they know they are somehow out of the game.

Gina fell in love also. (Woman call Yola).

Then the war came (different than before) and her love was taken in the battle. Or her love was taken by Home Office and deported forever on a plane.

G was alone then. Again.

Her dreams were calm though. With old Louise she sat in front of the TV w sound turned down and talked about her mum, the years she had missed back during her foolish and unfortunate youth as was spent largely uploaded to internet. Of details what happened to her there G still dint say much.

When time came (Miner's Strike) Louise also left (deceased). Then it was only Gina what lived there at the pub and she tired to continue, tried to continue in the life.

★

In keeping w the pub old old name (*George and The Dragon*) Gina bought a dragon one summer. They kept it out back, much as other pubs might in those days have placed a stupid or dangerous inflatable castle, just something bouncy bright/frivolous for the kids to play on while the rest got drunk during those Long Xtended Summer Months of the global warming.

The dragon itself was a large mournful creature in sick hues of grey green the opposite of vibrant. Scaled and once powerful, now indolent, tethered and real they said (the sellers) it was, according to their framed cert and the local paper writeup what G had proudly placed behind the bar, descended from the very same dragon that once upon a way back in the true true olden times of Endland had fought and been defeated by St George.

G started summer w all good intentions – to make the most of her purchase in business termz – and closely followed the instructions from a marketing webinar she had once attended. At her instruction a small marquee was erected near the dragon and meanwhile some tables was installed at the edge of the beer garden, up towards the overflow carpark in which the dragon was enclosed, long strings of new plastic flags being stretched taut, crisscrossing sky and barren tarmac like a celebration of the old Battle of Britain and leading back towards the pub.

Later G found a loose gaggle of neighbourhood teenagers to gather awkwardly at the folding camping table she bought from Argos and from which they could easily more or less run the show, charging entrance to the dragons' area for parents, grandparents etc of toddlers tirelessly desperate to clamber on what the signs said was a glorious and mighty beast, or for those more adventurass (sic) of them (the kids) to slide down its permanently cowed neck and land on the filthy crash mat below or for those even bolder to offer the miserable creature water from the set of six plastic buckets provided for that purpose.

As the heat of that summer rose month on month though the novelty of the dragon attraction wore pretty thin and there was neither the enthusiasm or the organisational infrastructure to maintain the setup it required – the ticket station was abandoned, the water tank run dry, the flags fell tangled in the blighted pervasive Endland rose bush and barbed wire, the britely coloured pendants trodden roughly into the heat-soft tarmac underfoot, while the dragon itself cowered daily and desperate up against the creosoted fence, ankles worn to bleeding by its chains, eyes lethargic, seeking shade and moaning loudly in a woeful broken and terminal distress at the edges of its crash-barrier enclosure.

G dint know what to do. There were some that tried to intervene – breaking off from their convos about the Brexit or the All New Yorkshire Ripper to throw chips out of sympathy to the beast or chucking sausage (with ketchup and also without) to it in theatrical gestures of simultaneous largesse and overwhelming disdain. But in truth in this fare the dragon just dint seem that interested and people themselves soon lost their interested too – WHO WANTS A PET THAT DON'T LIKE TREATS was the general opinion and folks just locked their kids in their cars and went back inside the pub where it was cooler anyway and easier to keep an eye on the football or latest instalment of *The Loveless Island*.

There were some meanwhile who complained the whole situation to authorities of course creating a fuss, as there will always be those that try to spoil things for everyone – citing cruelty to animals and crapping on to Gina in a series of threatening anonymous notes about rights and rights and wrongs of all things etc. But from a legalistic perspective the cops that came out to the pub one nite said that dragons weren't really real anyhows and that non-existent creatures were not covered by impact of the law, not fully not even partly in fact.

So by the time the autumn 1990 (?) came the dragon was all but forgotten and Gina as a total pragmatist sold it on to another pub further north, 50 quid/cash only/no questions and no one heard about it no more and things like quietened down.

Gina somehow missed the dragon tho. The look in its eyes she sympathise, the great shake that the walls of the pub used to make in the darkness of a midnight when it sighed, like the lorries thunder on the road they used to make out there before the bypass.

Late nites in the months after it was sold, when work was done she used to sit up all alone in the pub and stare out of the window, listening to the old Drill tunes of her youth and dreamed again repeatedly of her Internet wherin she had lived, loved and drifted so many years.

~~Place behind hills where each nite the many stars are fallen. That the sun, the stars, the heavens have fallen there.~~

~~He opened his eyes and taken from the beauty of the clothing of the princess, that he could hardly determine if it was a~~

~~dream or a reality. He him spoke first: she spoke to him in turn.~~

One morning the Gas Man came to read the meter at the pub and the whole place was found total empty, a meal set upon the table, all doors and windows ajar and a note left writ in Gina's best biro hand still jotted on the scrap paper next the telephone and the jar/blue plastic thing collecting coins for the poor kids and Cerebral Palsy. Note was part illegible but some could be discerned.

~~Cut from above. Let it go. Let fortune guide him. Her.~~
~~Do not try searching again. Sometimes things are buried for a reason.~~
~~Try saving again and again.~~
~~long fainting.~~
~~It was so strong that it brought back more.~~

When the cops eventually got involved there were just a few search parties thru G's search histories and a handful of like good old Babes in Uniform making door to door enquiries in the neighbourhood, running strict fingers thru G's long abandoned keywords, bookmarks and overflow caches, then just shrug and slowly walk away.

~~There is a forest in Endland.~~
~~There was once a forest of Endland.~~
~~she got up as soon as it was day, and ran towards the sea.~~

About the Editor

Catherine Taylor is a freelance writer, editor and critic for *The Guardian, FT Life and Arts, TLS* and the *New Statesman* among other publications, and commercial director of the *Brixton Review of Books*. Catherine was publisher at The Folio Society for over a decade and deputy director of freedom of expression charity English PEN from 2014-2016. She has judged several literary prizes including the Jewish-Quarterly Wingate, Guardian First Book Award, European Union Prize for Literature and most recently the Republic of Consciousness Prize for Small Presses. Catherine is currently writing *The Stirrings*, a cultural memoir of Sheffield.

About the Authors

Margaret Drabble was born in 1939 in Sheffield and educated at Newnham College, Cambridge. She had a very brief career as an actor with the Royal Shakespeare Company, before taking to fiction. Her first novel, *A Summer Birdcage,* was published in 1963, and her nineteenth and most recent, *The Dark Flood Rises,* in 2016. She also edited two editions of *The Oxford Companion to English Literature* (1985, 2000). She is married to the biographer Michael Holroyd and lives in London, Oxford and Somerset.

Tim Etchells is an artist and a writer based in the UK whose work shifts between performance, visual art and fiction. He has worked in a wide variety of contexts, notably as the leader of the world-renowned Sheffield-based performance group Forced Entertainment. Exhibiting and presenting work in significant institutions all over the world, he is currently Professor of Performance & Writing at Lancaster University. Tim's collection of short fiction *Endland* is published by And Other Stories (2019).

ABOUT THE AUTHORS

Naomi Frisby is a writer, interviewer and educator. Her story 'Role Play' was shortlisted for The White Review Short Story Prize and 'The Bodies' was longlisted for the Manchester Fiction Prize. She has written about books for a number of online publications including Ozy and Fiction Uncovered, and is the copywriter for Manchester Literature Festival. She regularly interviews writers at festivals and bookshops: her interviewees have included Jenny Eclair and Marcus Zusak. Naomi is completing a PhD in Creative Writing at Sheffield Hallam University focusing on female freaks in circus novels. Originally from Barnsley, South Yorkshire, she now lives in Sheffield.

Philip Hensher was born in 1965 and grew up in Sheffield. His novels set in Sheffield are *The Northern Clemency* (2008), shortlisted for the Man Booker Prize, *The Friendly Ones* (2018) and the forthcoming *A Small Revolution in Germany* (2020), from which 'Visiting the Radicals' is excerpted. He lives in South London and Geneva.

Helen Mort was born in Sheffield and grew up in Chesterfield. She has published two poetry collections, *Division Street* (2013) and *No Map Could Show Them* (2016), and one novel, *Black Car Burning* (2019). Her short story collection *Exire* was published by Wrecking Ball in 2019 and she also co-edited *One For The Road: Pubs and Poetry* (Smith-Doorstop) with Stuart Maconie. Helen teaches Creative Writing at Manchester Metropolitan University and is a Fellow of the Royal Society of Literature.

Geoff Nicholson was born in Sheffield on his grandmother's kitchen table in Hillsborough. He has had plays performed at the Edinburgh Festival and on BBC radio, and written comedy for Chris Tarrant among others. His works include

Bleeding London, The Lost Art of Walking, and *Footsucker*. He currently divides his time, unequally, between California and Essex.

Gregory Norminton is the author of five novels – most recently *The Devil's Highway* (Fourth Estate) – and two collections of short stories. *The Ghost Who Bled*, his second collection, was published by Comma Press in 2017. Gregory Norminton is a senior lecturer in Creative Writing at Manchester Metropolitan University. He lives in Sheffield with his wife and daughter.

Johny Pitts is a writer, photographer and broadcast journalist. He has received various awards for his work exploring African-European identity, including a Decibel Penguin Prize and an ENAR (European Network Against Racism) award. He is the curator of the online journal Afropean.com, part of the *Guardian*'s Africa Network and has collaborated with Caryl Philips on a photographic essay about London's immigrant communities for the BBC and Arts Council. *Afropean: Notes from Black Europe* was published by Penguin in 2019.

Désirée Reynolds is a writer, editor, activist and creative writing workshop facilitator, living in Sheffield. She has written film scripts, short stories and flash fiction. Her stories appear in various anthologies, both online and in print. *Seduce*, her first novel, was published to great acclaim by Peepal Tree Press in 2013, and her forthcoming second novel received support from Arts Council England. She is also the Editor of *Writing as Resistance*, an anthology of new writing funded by the University of Sheffield's Festival of the Mind.

Karl Riordan is a writer based in Sheffield. His first poetry collection, *The Tattooist's Chair,* was published by Smokestack

Books in 2017. He has an MA in Creative Writing from the University of Sheffield, and is working on a second collection of poems and a book of short stories. He is currently a Disability Support Worker and Library Assistant, but has previously worked as a barber, scrap-collector, teacher, and postal worker.

Special Thanks

At Comma Press: Ra Page, Sarah Cleave, Becca Parkinson and Zoe Turner. With special thanks to Sarah for her endless patience and forensic eye. Roz Dineen and Catharine Morris at the *Times Literary Supplement* and Rhiannon Lucy Cosslett at the *Guardian*, for commissioning my pieces on Sheffield past and present. Michael Caines, Will Eaves and our wonderful team at the *Brixton Review of Books*. John Haffenden and Sunjeev Sahota for encouraging my writing on Sheffield. Daniela Petracco, dearest friend. Sheffield co-conspirators over many years: Alex Henderson, Sonia Misak, Fiona Simic, Abi Amor and Sarah Castleton. Finally, my nephew Joseph Malcomson and my niece Jude Malcomson, the second generation of our family to grow up in the Steel City.

Catherine Taylor

The Book of Birmingham

Edited by Kavita Bhanot

'Each story provides its own rich, textured, and complex history of the city post-WWII to the present.'– *Rewrite London*

Few cities have undergone such a radical transformation over the last few decades as Birmingham. Culturally and architecturally, it has been in a state of perpetual flux and regeneration, with new communities moving in, then out, and iconic post-war landmarks making way for brighter-coloured, 21st century flourishes. Much like the city itself, the characters in the stories gathered here are often living through moments of profound change, closing in on a personal or societal turning point, that carries as much threat as it does promise.

Set against key moments of history – from Malcolm X's visit to Smethwick in 1965, to the Handsworth riots two decades later, from the demise of the city's manufacturing in the 70s and 80s, to the on-going tensions between communities in recent years – these stories celebrate the cultural dynamism that makes this complex, often divided 'second city' far more than just the sum of its parts.

Featuring: Balvinder Banga, Alan Beard, Jendella Benson, Kit de Waal, Sharon Duggal, Joel Lane, Malachi McIntosh, Bobby Nayyar, C.D. Rose & Sibyl Ruth

ISBN: 978-1-91097-437-7
£9.99

The Book of Leeds

Edited by Maria Crossan & Tom Palmer

Millgarth Police Station reverberates with the early adrenalin-rush of a case they won't close for years.

A teenage boy trails the city centre bars of the eighties in thrall to his hero – a Leeds United football hooligan.

A single woman finds her frustrations with men confirmed speed-dating in a city re-invented as a party capital.

Bringing together fiction from some of the city's most celebrated writers, The Book of Leeds traces the unique contours that fifty years of social and economic change can impress on a city. These are stories that take place at oblique angles to the larger events in the city's history, or against wider currents that have shaped the social and cultural landscape of today's Leeds: a modern city with both problems and promise.

Featuring: M.Y. Alam, Martyn Bedford, Ian Duhig, Jeremy Dyson, Susan Everett, Tony Harrison, Shamshad Khan, Tom Palmer, David Peace & Andrea Semple

ISBN: 978-1-90558-301-0
£9.99